4.95
2.95
D92

Exit Actors,
Dying

Other Penny Spring and Sir Toby Glendower Mysteries

MARGOT ARNOLD

Exit Actors, Dying

A Penny Spring and Sir Toby Glendower Mystery

A Foul Play Press Book

The Countryman Press
Woodstock, Vermont

This edition is published in 1988 by Foul Play Press, a division
of The Countryman Press, Woodstock, Vermont 05091.

ISBN 0-88150-115-8

Printed in the United States of America

WHO'S WHO

GLENDOWER, TOBIAS MERLIN, archaeologist, F.B.A., F.S.A., K.B.E.; b. Swansea, Wales, Dec. 27, 1926; s. Thomas Owen and Myfanwy (Williams) G.; ed. Winchester Coll.; Magdalen Coll., Oxford, B.A., M.A., Ph.D.; fellow Magdalen Coll., 1949-; prof. Near Eastern and European Prehistoric Archaeology Oxford U., 1964-; created Knight, 1977. Participated in more than 30 major archaeological expeditions. Author publications, including: What Not to Do in Archaeology, 1960; What to Do in Archaeology, 1970; also numerous excavation and field reports. Clubs: Old Wykehamists, Athenaeum, Wine-tasters, University.

SPRING, PENELOPE ATHENE, anthropologist; b. Cambridge, Mass., May 16, 1928; d. Marcus and Muriel (Snow) Thayer; B.A., M.A., Radcliffe Coll.; Ph.D., Columbia U.; m. Arthur Upton Spring, June 24, 1953 (dec.); 1 son, Alexander Marcus. Lectr. anthropology Oxford U., 1958-68; Mathieson Reader in anthropology Oxford U., 1969-; fellow St. Anne's Coll., Oxford, 1969-. Field work in the Marquesas, East and South Africa, Uzbekistan, India, and among the Pueblo, Apache, Crow and Fox Indians. Author: Sex in the South Pacific, 1957; The Position of Women in Pastoral Societies, 1962; And Must They Die? —A Study of the American Indian, 1965; Caste and Change, 1968; Moslem Women, 1970; Crafts and Culture, 1972; The American Indian in the Twentieth Century, 1974; Hunter vs. Farmer, 1976.

CHAPTER 1

Penelope Spring leaned back in her theater seat with a sigh of contentment. She felt warm and relaxed and—further bliss—had the whole theater completely to herself. From where she sat, halfway up the great hemisphere, the steeply tiered rows of marble seats fell away like a frozen cascade to the dark-green semicircle of the grassy stage below. Behind it and the jagged broken columns of its proscenium arch was the most spectacular backdrop of any theater in the world, the Vale of Pergamum, just wakening now from winter sleep and shimmering faintly emerald in the sunlight as it stretched away to misty blue hills on the far horizon. Above these hills lay a line of threatening nimbus clouds, the somber purple of ripe grapes, and, even as she watched, a sharp flash of lightning illuminated their sullen underbellies. But for the moment Zeus was content to hurl his thunderbolts afar. There was no threat to his own Great Altar, which lay in magnificent ruin farther up the hill behind her, nor to his theater, which was hers for the moment—the most perfect theater in the world, the Ionian Greeks had claimed, and she was prepared to believe them. Above her, still, the sky was a steady cerulean blue; here, all was peace and sunshine.

She would go and explore Zeus's altar and the temples later on, much later on, she decided—just so long as she could give it a quick once-over before Toby Glendower gave her the "scientist's tour." She had learned long ago that to sight-see with him was to be so bombarded by expert knowledge that, in order to have any recollection of the places as places, she had to do what she was doing now—take a sneak preview as a mere human being.

But not just yet, she thought comfortably. *I'll just sit here awhile and bask.* She closed her eyes and gave another immense sigh of satisfaction. How gorgeous it was to be away from England and rain and students and anthropology and Oxford—much as she loved them all—for three glorious weeks. The delight was compounded by the fact that she knew she ought to be in Philadelphia attending the Wenner-Grenn conference with her fellow anthropologists, delivering herself of her latest weighty brainchild, and not bucketing around Turkey with an eccentric archaeologist who had more money than was good for him. So, to warmth and delight was added a most delicious sense of guilt.

A small rustling noise indicated that the seat next to her had just been taken, and she opened one eye to see a small brown lizard sprawled at his ease there. The fawn brown of his back mottled imperceptibly into pale primrose on his underside and head, which was turned toward her. His watchful, beady red eyes regarded her. His pale-yellow throat was palpitating nervously, but he stood his ground and, deciding that Penny presented no threat, settled down to bask contentedly beside her.

Having assimilated with appreciation the small perfection of his form, Penny was about to close her eye when a movement far below caught her outer field of vision—a flash of white and gold against a gray pillar—and she opened the other eye to see what this might be. The greensward of the stage remained unsullied, and nothing else moved in all the huge semicircle of marble; yet she sensed rather than saw that there had been movement of some kind below. A faint whisper of sound reached her ears and seemed momentarily to grow in volume. The Greeks had claimed that the acoustics here were so perfect a pin dropped upon the stage could be heard in the farthest tier, and she was prepared to believe that, too. *Oh, damn,* she thought crossly, *I don't want to share this with anyone. Perhaps if I ignore them, they'll leave me in peace.* She closed her eyes again with determination, as the lizard beside her basked unconcernedly on.

Who could it be? Penny wondered idly. It was too early in the season for the usual tourist hordes. When she and Toby had arrived at the small hotel in modern Bergama last night, they had been its only foreign guests. Besides, it was a good five kilometers from the modern town to the ancient city here on the hill, as her cab driver had taken pains to inform her when he brought her this morning and eagerly offered to come back and fetch her at noon. She had heard no sound of any other vehicle on the dirt road below, but, then, she had not really been listening. The faint sounds diminished and then died away altogether. She smiled contentedly to herself and lifted her face to the benison of the sun. Peace returned. *I should get one of those reflector things and get a real tan,* she was thinking cozily when a startled "Tchrrk" and a rustling indicated she had just lost her little companion.

She opened her eyes to see the small, pointed tail disappearing into a crevice in the marble seat, and again a flash of white and gold caught her eye. She looked down toward the stage and caught her breath. She was no longer alone.

Lying near one of the central pillars at the back of the green stage was the figure of a girl, dressed in a white tunic embroidered in gold. The sun flashed from golden sandals, and it looked for all the world like a figure left over from one of the Greek tragedies that had been played out on this stage two thousand years before. The figure did not move, but one white arm was stretched artistically before it on the grass, the head pillowed in its curve.

Penny glanced around, half expecting to see some long-haired young man with a long-nosed camera busily snapping fashion shots, but apart from herself and the still figure on the stage there was no one. Her curiosity piqued, she got up and began a rather undignified scramble down the towering, tiered structure. *Odd place for a nap,* she reflected, since her progress was far from noiseless and yet the figure never stirred. Finally reaching the green turf of the stage and panting slightly with her efforts, Penny surveyed the sleeper.

The clothing might have been taken straight off a Greek vase, she thought, even the thongs of the sandals were authentic in design—but the wearer was something else again! Penny had seen many beauties from Grecian art, but nothing to touch this girl: the legs and body were divine, and the face and hair out of this world, but the beauty was not that of the dark and olive hues of the South, but rather of the cream-and-gold delicacy of the North. The girl, in fact, was probably the most perfect specimen of the Nordic type she had ever seen. The hair was like purest spun gold, the skin creamy white with a delicate peach flush on the cheeks, and Penny was positive that the eyes, when they opened, would be a pure azure blue. Her own eyes traveled slowly over the perfect form. How Toby would appreciate this rare *objet d'art,* she was thinking wryly when, for the first time, she became aware of a most ominous fact. This rare Nordic flower was not breathing.

For a moment she could not believe her eyes; but there was no doubt about it: no breath of life remained to trouble those perfect lips. Penny stooped over and gingerly felt the girl's arm; it still felt warm to her touch.

Of course, she muttered crossly to herself. *How could she have been here long? Corpses don't walk into the middle of a stage and lie down while you are taking a few seconds' doze in the back balcony. She must have been alive when she lay down. But what did she die of? If it was a heart attack, surely she would be blue around the lips, or twisted, or something.* Penny's hand strayed to the petallike cheek and in so doing dislodged the head from its resting place on the outstretched arm. It fell forward, and a lock of golden hair slid out of place, leaving part of the neck visible. Penny recoiled sharply. Just at the base of the skull was a long, narrow wound, the blood already drying around the edges. It did not take a second glance to know that this was no accidental injury. It was a stab wound inflicted by some long, thin object. Her lips set grimly. No one could conceivably inflict a wound like *that* on themselves. This lovely creature had obviously been murdered!

Firmly quelling a rising tide of panic, Penny tried to collect her thoughts. Now what should she do? It seemed wrong somehow to leave this beautiful thing lying as she was—the focal point of thousands of ghostly eyes from all those empty tiers—and yet she knew enough not to move the body. It would mean the local Turkish police, of course, and she wondered ethnocentrically how ably they would cope with such an exceedingly bizarre occurrence.

But first she had to get to them. A glance at her watch showed her it was only ten-thirty; her taxi would not be here for at least another hour and a half. Too long to wait and wonder. She would just have to walk the five kilometers and hope to pick up a lift of some kind once she had got down to the base of the hill and the main road.

As soon as her mind was made up, she started toward one of the side exits on the stage, knowing from her earlier explorations that she could get from there to the long tunnel that led to the ancient dressing rooms and to the lower exits of the great theater. As she moved, a motion from above brought her to a frozen halt. She looked up, and a scream bubbled to her lips, but it emerged more like the squeak of a startled bat. There, standing behind the back row of seats she had so recently vacated, towered a giant figure of superhuman proportions, clad incredibly in the full regalia of a Roman gladiator; and, most terrifying of all, beneath the gladiatorial helmet and visor, the sun reflected only a blank blackness. As Penny watched in paralyzed fascination, the ghostly figure raised its sword in the Roman gesture of farewell, stepped backward and disappeared from view.

For a second she stood rooted with terror, and then, with one final apologetic glance at the still figure on the grass, she ran as fast as she could into the gloom of the tunnel and again into the bright sunlight outside of the theater. Too terrified to look behind her, she scuttled down the track that led to the main road. On reaching it, she looked up and down, desperate for something, anything, with wheels or legs that could carry her away from the horrors on the hill. But this was simply not destined to be her day. Not so much as a donkey was in sight. Lips grimly set, she started to jog determinedly toward her distant goal, hoping with fervor that the giant ghostly gladiator had more pressing business elsewhere and was not bearing down on her undefended rear.

It didn't help, she thought as she stumbled doggedly onward, to be forty-eight years old, five-foot-one, and a dumpy five-foot-one at that. Her romantic-minded archaeologist father had always dreamed of a slim and willowy maiden, rosy and fleet of foot. He had even toyed with the idea of calling his sole offspring Atalanta—or so her mother had informed her—but, faced with the uncompromisingly short, square baby she had been, he had sadly compromised on Penelope Athene. For once Penny wished fervently she *had* been the girl of her father's dreams and would thus be eating up the miles with the fleetness and lightness of the fabulous Atalanta. As it was, she had to make do with what she had, which was precious little, and so she kept pantingly on until, finally, the vision of the white hotel with its pale-blue trim rose before her sweat-dimmed eyes.

With a final burst of energy she flung herself through the door and, hurdling the mounds of luggage that were unexpectedly strewn around the normally empty entrance lounge, raced up to the startled young assistant manager behind the reception desk. She sagged against the counter, eyes glazed, hopelessly disheveled and pouring with sweat. With what she was positive must be her last gasp, she sobbed out, "Get the police, the police. I've got to report a murder." Then her knees buckled under her, and she disappeared from view, sliding to the floor in a small, panting heap. There she found herself gazing at a pale-pink Samsonite case bearing a label that announced in an elaborate Gothic script,

MELODY MARTIN, SCROWSKI PRODUCTIONS
HOLLYWOOD, ROME, MARSEILLES

The cautious head of the assistant manager peered anxiously over the edge of the counter. "Did you say *murder?*"

"Indeed I did," said Penelope Athene Spring.

CHAPTER 2

Decidedly this was not her day, Penny thought. She was sitting in the back of a jeep, tightly wedged between the local chief of police, who was glowering suspiciously at her, and his younger assistant, who, fortunately for her, had turned out to be fluent in English. The jeep was careening at breakneck speed back over the road she had so lately and so painfully traversed. The resultant bumping was so horrendous that she had one hand firmly clamped on the back of the driver's seat to brace herself for what she was sure was going to be an accident, as the other tried vainly to keep her sweat-soaked locks out of her eyes. Double pneumonia for sure, she predicted crossly, and where in the world had Toby got to? How like a man! Always underfoot when they weren't particularly needed and never around in a crisis. She was totally reliant on him as translator, knowing only a few basic phrases of Turkish herself. Though he had been hunted for high and low, not a trace of him had been found, and she had had to go to the police headquarters without him. She didn't know what she would have done if it hadn't been for the young man beside her. She could never have recounted her weird experience to the chief of police, who obviously belonged to the old Turkish school of thought that regarded all foreigners as objects of the deepest suspicion, and foreign women in particular as something spawned in hell. She glanced gratefully at the slim, neat young man on her left, and he responded with a flash of his large, dark eyes and a sympathetic grin.

It was he who had answered the summons to the hotel and who had accompanied her to the police station, where he had acted as a most efficient bumper between her—in a frenzy of impatience for something to be done—and the chief of police, who had rapidly passed from a polite disbelief in her story to an angry disbelief.

He had seemed far more interested in minutely examining with a maddening slowness her own credentials and had found in every line of them fuel for his deepening suspicions.

Why, if she were an American, as her passport claimed, did she live in England? he had demanded. She worked there, she explained through her sturdy interpreter, and, besides, her husband had been an Englishman.

It said she was a widow, so who was this man she was said to be with? A colleague who worked with her at the university and with whom she always traveled. The chief, who evidently thought that widows should be discreetly draped in black and keep to the house as much as possible, took this very hard. Where was this man? he demanded, and Toby's absence from her side added another black mark.

Her occupation of anthropologist had to be explained to him, and he immediately and belligerently asked to know what primitive people she expected to find in *this* part of Turkey. Hastily disclaiming any desire to do fieldwork, she had explained—patiently, she thought—that she was merely looking at the many ancient sites with her friend, who was an archaeologist.

They were, perhaps, looking for a site to excavate? he suggested craftily. Remembering some of the more unfortunate encounters between English archaeologists and Turkish officialdom, she firmly vetoed this idea and reiterated that they were only tourists and had planned to visit most of the major sites throughout Turkey during the period of their visitor's visas. They had already been to Antioch, Mersin, Izmir and now . . .

No doubt they had also visited their old U.S. NATO bases, too, he had put in slyly.

At this she had exploded. No, they most certainly had not, and she didn't like his tone one little bit. They were here first, last and always as *tourists,* and while he was sitting there trying to make something out of nothing, there happened to be the rapidly cooling body of a murdered woman lying up in the Greek theater, and what, if anything, was he proposing to do about *that?*

And so, finally, they had got under way. Now the jeep drew up in a cloud of dust and squealing brakes at one of the lower exits of the Greek theater.

Acutely aware of her aching and rapidly stiffening limbs, Penny climbed clumsily out, only to be told to stay where she was until they had examined the scene of the crime. They disappeared into the long subterranean tunnel, leaving the driver of the car gazing gloomily but fixedly at her. The swift ride had chilled her, so under his disapproving gaze she trotted up and down in the sun to warm herself and to get some of the kinks out.

Soon the assistant chief of police reappeared at the tunnel's mouth. He looked worried. "Please come," he said.

She followed his neat khaki back into the darkness and once more emerged in blinding sunlight. The police chief was standing in the middle of the stage, his short, stocky body alive with anger, his broad shoulders hunched forward and his swarthy face like a thundercloud. As she stumbled toward him, momentarily blinded by the sun, he ripped off a stream of Turkish, which the young man haltingly translated.

"He says that it is no light matter to make fools of the Turkish police and that, unless you have some very good explanation for this fool's errand we have come on, he is going to arrest you and throw you in jail."

"What?" Penny said blankly, and then, gazing frantically around at the empty green stage, "What have you done with the body?"

"There *was* no body—nothing at all," the assistant said.

Penny ran to the gray pillar and looked desperately around, but the golden girl was gone. "But there *was* a body," she yelled, "right here!"

The young man shook his head slowly. "There was nothing here, and nobody—nobody at all." His hands sketched in the emptiness of the theater.

"Then, he must have come back and hidden her somewhere. You must search," Penny said vehemently.

"He? Who?"

She had not told them of the spectral gladiator. She had wanted to be in the theater, to be able to show rather than tell them what had happened, and she had wanted to check on something herself before she did so. Hastily she now explained all this to the young Turk, who looked searchingly at her before passing it along to his chief. It did nothing to improve the latter's temper.

"Is this American mad, Bilger?" he demanded. "What does she say of this nonexistent murdered body? Ask her why there is no blood, no sign."

"No, I do not think she is mad, Hamit Bey," Bilger said cautiously. "Why would she tell such a fantastic story? I think she really believes something has happened here, but we must find out more. Show us where the body was," he said, turning to Penny, who obliged and then, carefully avoiding the actual spot, demonstrated how the body had been lying.

"Then, why is there no blood?" he demanded.

"Because obviously she wasn't killed here," Penny said thoughtfully. Their doubting attitude was helping to clarify her own thinking, and lying here on the grass took her mind off her own body's aches and pains. "The body was still warm, so she couldn't have been dead long, and there was no sign of rigor mortis, but the blood around the stab wound was already starting to darken and dry. It wasn't even oozing, so that's why there is no evidence of it on the grass."

"There's no evidence that *anything* has been on the grass," he said emphatically.

"But she *was* here. Look around. There must be something to indicate she was here," Penny said with increasing desperation. From her prone position on the ground, she squinted along it; toward the right exit tunnel a faint glitter of gold caught her eye. She scrambled to her feet with an eager cry and pounced on the object, which was almost invisible from an upright position. It was a small piece of gold trimming. She held it out to them excitedly as a whole new host of possibilities flooded her mind. "Look, this is off her dress—I'd swear to it! It was trimmed with gold in a Greek-key design; I remember thinking how pretty it was. And it's American—I'd almost swear to that, too—the sort of thing you can find in any American chain store."

Bilger handed the small scrap over to Hamit Bey, who was examining it from every angle as if it were a faceted diamond.

"Why do you say that?" Bilger demanded.

"Because," Penny said slowly, "I've got an idea who these people might be. It's just an idea mind you, but they may be actors. That would explain the odd clothing they wore. While I was waiting for you at the hotel, I noticed a pile of luggage with a film company's name on it. They may be coming here to make a film. That's something you could easily check."

"But you said the gladiator had no face and that he just vanished," Bilger said dubiously.

"I know, but it may have been a trick of the sunlight—about the face, I mean—or he may have been wearing some sort of mask. Anyway, let's check about where he was standing." Penny led the way up the steep aisle of the theater, stopping to point out where she had been sitting and then to where the giant had appeared and disappeared.

When she gained the corridor circling around the back row of seats, her suspicions about his fast disappearance were borne out: a square, dark hole containing a steep flight of steps running in a counter direction to the main banks of seats was disclosed. "An old exit for the upper tiers, I suppose," she pointed out. "It probably leads to a corridor running underneath the whole of the back of the circle and linking up with the other tunnels."

"So you claim this gladiator must have stabbed the girl with the sword he waved at you?" Bilger queried.

"No, I don't think so," Penny said hesitantly. "If it was a genuine Roman sword—or, rather, a replica of one—it would have been too broad to inflict the wound I saw. But, as I recall, gladiators also were equipped with thin-bladed daggers, and it was more like a dagger wound."

"How is it that you know so much about all this?" Bilger asked suavely. "Types of wounds and rigor mortis and so on. Surely such things are not within an anthropologist's scope, are they?" He looked at her curiously.

"Well, no . . ." Penny was defensive. "But I think you'd find that any layman knows about these things nowadays, what with all the crime shows on television and so on." She did not like to add that she had been an avid reader of mystery stories from the age of ten and, as a result, could make an accurate diagnosis of far more tricky deaths than a simple stab wound. He continued to look at her curiously, and she felt now was the time to make a direct and weak-womanly appeal to him. She put a small, confiding hand on his arm and said earnestly, "Look, I'm not raving mad, and I have no sinister motives for all this. I *saw* exactly what I have told you—no more, no less. You *do* believe me, don't you?"

He nodded his head slowly. "Yes. Although there is practically nothing to back up your story, I'm inclined to believe you—principally because of the state you were in when I first saw you in the hotel. If you were making all this up, you could just as well have waited until the cab driver came for you. However, I'm afraid my chief doesn't share my views." He looked over to where Hamit Bey was now pacing up and down muttering to himself. A glance at her watch confirmed Penny's suspicion that his impatience was not unallied to the fact it was now well past lunchtime. Bilger joined him, exchanged a low-voiced remark and then returned to her side. "If you'd return to the car with him, I'll just have a quick look around, and then we'll go back to town."

But the dejected stoop of his shoulders when he eventually did rejoin them told her that his search had yielded nothing tangible to add to the credibility of her story or to the single, slender bit of evidence—the scrap of gold braid.

They drove back to town in grim silence, but, on reaching the hotel, a longer and more heated conversation took place between Bilger and the fuming chief. Penny awaited the outcome with anxiety. She was feeling extremely weary and in most urgent need of a long, hot bath, and the prospect of being hauled off to the dubious comforts of a Turkish jail was profoundly unattractive. She was therefore immeasurably relieved when Bilger finally turned to her with a faint smile and said, "At least for the moment I have persuaded the chief not to arrest you. I pointed out to him that you would undoubtedly contact the American consul in Izmir if he took such a step, and, as you may imagine, he is not very anxious to face the repercussions of that. So you are free until I have had an opportunity to make some more inquiries—about this film company and so on. But I must advise you to stick closely to the hotel and, above all, do not try to leave Bergama until this has been cleared up—not for any reason. For the moment, good-bye, *Bayan* Spring. If you remember anything else or have anything else to add, please contact me direct; Bilger Kosay is my name."

An hour later found Penny bathed, reclothed and groomed into some semblance of a human being, sitting before her sixth cup of Turkish coffee in the empty hotel dining room. The coffee had been a mistake. Instead of soothing and warming, it had stimulated and set every nerve in her body to jangling. She was feeling extremely bad-tempered, her mind a whirl of chaotic thoughts and apprehensions.

Whichever way she looked at this dismal situation, she failed to see any hint of a silver lining. At worst she'd land in jail, and at best it looked as if her much-looked-forward-to holiday plans were blown to smithereens. Her bad temper was augmented by the knowledge that Toby would certainly not take kindly to any of this.

The worst thing about long-term bachelors was that they were so set in their ways, she thought moodily, and Toby had more than his fair share of hang-ups to begin with. It came of having such an extraordinary childhood and too much money. She realized it was no fault of his that his father—besides being a money-maker of no mean ability—had been a wild-eyed fanatic on the subject of Welsh nationalism and, for that matter, all things Welsh and wonderful. No wonder the word *Celt* to Toby was like a red flag to a bull!

As a compensation for the thorough brainwashing of his childhood, Toby had become almost an equal fanatic in other directions, becoming as pro-Greek (the ancient kind) as his father was pro-Welsh. In addition to this, he had the uncertain temperament allied to near genius, a photographic memory, and a peculiar gift for languages. So he lived and built his life around the Mediterranean past and filled the few gaps that remained with his vast esoteric "collections" and—she grimaced wryly—drinking. Wine drinking mostly, but on a scale that would have made Rabelais envious.

Putting it all together made for the most fascinating human being she had ever encountered—but not an easy one, definitely not easy.

And where the hell is he? she was saying to herself for the hundredth time when the door of the dining room opened and the round, moonlike face of Tobias M. (for Merlin) Glendower peered cautiously around it.

"Where the devil have you *been!*" she exploded, overwhelmed with relief at the sight of him.

The head made a shushing noise, and the long, lanky body inserted itself into the room and closed the door carefully behind it. Toby Glendower sloped toward her with the dazed air of a man who has just been hit with a sledgehammer.

His only claim to physical beauty was his hair, which was plentiful and a distinguished silver gray. His face and head were impossibly round and small, sitting like a knob on top of a long, thin body, mostly composed of leg, which was bowed into almost a parody of a scholar's stoop. Round blue eyes gazed lugubriously out of equally round glasses, and the small mouth, which was generally sucking on the stem of a pipe, added to his air of being an elderly, sad baby.

Now, however, the round blue eyes were panic-stricken, and the mouth opened in an *O* of silent protest.

"Well!" Penny said crossly. "I suppose you've heard the awful news, but you'd better hear my side of it before you say anything."

He did not seem to hear her but instead bent toward her and whispered urgently, "I'm going to need your help, Penny. Something most unfortunate has happened." He paused dramatically. "I've found a body—"

Penny jumped to her feet in excitement. "Oh, great! You've found it; you've found my body! Oh, that's wonderful!"

"*Your* body?" he muttered dazedly.

"Yes, yes. Oh, you don't know what a relief this is. Where is she?"

"She?" he echoed, stupefied.

"Oh, for God's sake, Toby, don't just stand there repeating everything I say. We've got to let Bilger Kosay know at once. Where did you find my Greek-costumed blonde?"

Toby suddenly came to life. "It wasn't a she," he roared. "It was a he—a bloody great Negro togged out as a gladiator and as dead as mutton. What the hell are *you* talking about?"

They gazed at one another aghast. "You mean—we've got *two* bodies?" Penny muttered weakly.

"You mean, you too . . . ?" he stammered. She nodded. "And who the devil is Bilger Kosay?" he was saying when the door behind him opened and the young policeman stood framed within it, smiling at them. "Did someone mention my name?" he asked cheerfully.

They gazed at him in a dazed silence, and then Penny said in a strangled voice. "You'd better come in and sit down. We've got something to tell you."

CHAPTER 3

"Where on earth did you get to, and how did you land up here?" Penny hissed in Toby's ear. She had taken advantage of a momentary lull in the proceedings to draw him out of earshot, away from the crowd of officials clustered around the body.

Their surroundings echoed in a more solid and uninspired fashion the setting of her morning's adventure, but now the gray marble tiers of seats encompassed them on all sides, and the grass underfoot ran in a perfect oval to form a wide arena. They were in the Roman amphitheater of ancient Pergamum, sitting stolidly in its little valley a mile outside the ancient town. Whoever or whatever the giant gladiator had been, the setting for his exit could scarcely have been more appropriate. All that had been lacking at his death was the packed rows of bloodthirsty spectators cheering the giant's fall.

"I was *hiding*," Toby hissed back. He made a dismissive gesture with his hand. "Oh, it's too complicated to tell you about now—I'll fill you in later—but I was cornered by a most *frightful* woman at the hotel. She scared me half to death; so I thought this would be a good place to spend the morning, because she wouldn't dream of looking for me here. Anyway, I came and, well, I must have dozed off, what with the sun and everything."

"You brought a bottle with you," Penny said accusingly.

"Well—certainly I did," Toby said loftily. "After all, one of the objects of this trip was to see if any of the local wines were good enough to take home. You can't buy wine without *tasting* it, you know!"

"What was it?" Penny said coldly.

"A bottle of red Kavaklidere," he muttered.

"And you drank it all, I suppose."

"It was very good," he said defensively.

She sniffed. "I see. Well, go on."

"I suppose the shots awakened me. Three of them, I believe. I was sort of dazed—"

"I'm not surprised," Penny said.

He chose to ignore that and went on hurriedly, "Anyway, I just sat still for a minute or two. I was in the prefect's box over there, er, lying down, and when I got up, the first thing I saw was this gladiator lying out in the middle of the arena—not another soul in sight. I was so staggered I just stood there for a minute, but then I saw that he was moving slightly; so I vaulted the balustrade and ran over to him."

"You mean he was still alive!" Penny broke in.

Toby nodded grimly. "Yes, even though he had three bullets in him, he was alive and trying to crawl toward his sword, which was lying a couple of yards away, as if it had fallen out of his hand when he went down. As I got to him, he tried to heave himself up. An expression of great surprise came over his face when he saw me, his mouth worked, and a terrible sort of *urgent* look came into his eyes. He managed to get one word out, and then"—Toby swallowed hard—"blood just gushed out of his mouth, and he rolled over and died."

"What did he say?" Penny said breathlessly.

"Just the one word, *mammoth*," Toby said with puzzlement, then lapsed into silence.

"Mammoth? Are you sure?"

"Yes, positive. Although I was pretty shaken up, the word was quite clear."

"What on earth could it mean?"

Toby shrugged. "If you'd seen his eyes, you'd know it meant *something*, but what? Unless the murderer's somebody called Mammoth, which doesn't seem very likely," he added gloomily.

"You know, there is something about him that's vaguely familiar," Penny said thoughtfully. "I think I'll try and get another look." She sidled over and peered between the Turkish officials as Toby loped over to the terraced rows and sat down, taking out his pipe and stuffing tobacco into it with an abstracted air.

Penny rejoined him. "Yes, I think I know who he is," she muttered. "He's an American, a football player called

—called Washington Thompson," she finished triumphantly.

Toby regarded her with mild astonishment. "How on earth do you know that?"

"Oh, through Alexander. He gets *Sports Illustrated,* an American sports magazine. When he went off to Johns Hopkins, he never changed his address, and they still keep coming to the house. So, well, I generally look through them before stacking them away until he gets home."

Toby sniffed expressively, since he steadfastly maintained that she spoiled her one and only child. "And is there something special about this Washington Thompson?"

"Yes." She wrinkled her brow. "As you saw, he's very big—about seven feet, I think—but he was too heavy for basketball; so one of the pro-football teams used him as a back. He specialized in something—blocking kicks, perhaps. And there was something else about him, some scandal—oh, I *wish* I could remember what it was!"

"But what's he doing here? If he's a football player, what is he doing with a picture company, *if* that's what they are?"

"Oh, that's not so surprising. A lot of professional athletes act in their off season," Penny said vaguely, "O.J. Simpson and Joe Namath and, oh, just heaps. Besides, I don't think he is in football anymore—" She broke off as a worried-looking Bilger approached them.

He stopped, cleared his throat nervously, then said, "I'm afraid I have to ask you to come back to the station with us."

"But why?" Penny burst out. "We've both given you our full statements. We can't tell you anything more, and I'm worn out. This must surely banish all Hamit Bey's doubts that I was just imagining things this morning. I'm positive that *this* murdered man is the one I saw at the Greek theater."

Bilger looked increasingly unhappy. "I'm afraid it is not as simple as that. You see, Hamit Bey now thinks that you and *Bay* Glendower here are in collusion and that you tried to feed us a—what do you call it?—red herring earlier to cover up *this* crime."

"But that's ridiculous!" Penny stormed. "Why on earth

should we do such a thing? We've never set eyes on either of them before. Why doesn't the police chief look into the film company or whatever it is they were with? Obviously, it is far more likely to be something to do with *them*. I mean, we're not a pair of homicidal maniacs on the loose —just a pair of garden variety university professors."

"I know, I know," Bilger said sympathetically. "But things have been happening so fast we've not had time to get our bearings yet, and since you both apparently were on the spot when the murders occurred, well . . ." He shrugged.

"Then, you do believe in the other murder now?" Penny said quickly. "Have you found any trace of the girl—at least any trace of what he did with the body?"

Bilger shook his head slowly, opened his mouth, closed it again, as if struggling with a difficult decision, and then burst out, "There was one strange thing. The Negro had on under his armor an ordinary T-shirt with a breast pocket. There was something in it." He fumbled in his pocket and drew out a small glassine envelope and held it out for their inspection. Nestled inside the envelope was a tiny circular piece of glass, tinted blue.

"What on earth's that?" Penny said blankly.

"I know what it is." Toby's deep voice rumbled over her shoulder. "It's a contact lens—the sort that a brown-eyed person would wear to turn his eyes blue."

They gazed at one another in blank amazement as Hamit Bey stalked purposefully toward them. "They will come with us," he barked at Bilger. "And as soon as we find where he has hidden the gun, we will arrest them both."

Penny and Toby sat unhappily side by side on straight wooden chairs. Behind the closed door of Hamit Bey's office rose the sounds of heated argument.

"We're in a terrible fix," Penny whispered. "Do you think we should call for outside help? I mean, once they arrest us, we'll *really* be in a mess."

Toby made a soothing noise deep in his throat. "I think I can talk Hamit Bey out of that—once I get in to see him, that is—but what worries me is that they probably won't let us leave Bergama before this thing is cleared up. No, I think there is really only one thing for us to do if we are going to salvage this vacation."

"And what's that?" Penny asked hopefully.

"We'll just have to solve the murders ourselves."

"*Us*? But we wouldn't have the faintest idea how to go about it!"

"Why not?" Toby was positively complacent. "We are two highly intelligent human beings, trained to observe and deduce things. The methods used in both archaeology and anthropology are extremely similar to those used in criminology. Besides, if, as we suspect, the crimes are connected with a group of foreigners, *we* are more likely to find out what is going on than the Turks are."

"Well, you don't have to be so pompous about it," Penny said crossly. "How would we ever begin? There don't seem to be any more physical clues around, and we don't know any of the people involved."

"Then, we'll have to *get* to know them," Toby said firmly. "But for that we'll need to have our liberty and be able to get back to the hotel to do some snooping on our own account."

"And just how do you propose to change Hamit Bey's opinion that we are murderers number one and two?" Penny demanded acidly.

"Oh, I have some ideas," Toby murmured. "Sometimes my trick memory does have its uses—"

He was prevented from enlarging on this by the opening of Hamit Bey's door. A flustered-looking Bilger emerged. Toby uncoiled himself from the chair and stalked purposefully past Bilger into Hamit Bey's office. As he disappeared, Penny heard him intone a mellifluous string of Turkish, which she assumed correctly to be an elaborate greeting.

"What's he doing?" Bilger inquired suspiciously.

"Bearding the lion in his den," Penny said, but the idiom was too much for Bilger, who gazed at her blankly for a second and then hurried off.

Penny fidgeted on her chair as Toby's rich baritone droned on. He was using what she always thought of as his Richard Burton voice, calculated to charm the birds off trees in normal circumstances. Unfortunately, Hamit Bey was no bird. Still, so far so good, Toby as yet had not been forcibly ejected. Penny gave herself up to gloomy contemplation.

After a considerable interval, the door opened and the two men emerged. Penny was staggered to see that Hamit Bey was smiling and actually shook Toby's hand as the latter ripped off an equally flowery farewell.

Toby came over to her, looking like the Cheshire cat. "We're free to go back to the hotel," he informed her smugly.

"How did you manage it, for Pete's sake?"

"Just let's get out of here before he has second thoughts and I'll tell you," he rumbled, taking a firm grip on her elbow and guiding her past the curiously staring policemen.

"Well?" she demanded, once safely outside.

"Hamit Bey is quite a noted oenologist," Toby said blandly. "We met on common ground."

"An oeno—oh, a *wine* lover! And he let you go on the strength of that?"

"Well, my name was not unknown to him, particularly after I brought some of my more noted articles to his attention and praised some of his." Toby smirked. "But, anyway, it wasn't entirely on the strength of that. I pointed out one or two interesting facts to him, which opened up some avenues of investigation away from ourselves."

"Such as?" Penny prompted.

"I suggested, for instance, that he might want to have a complete autopsy done on our deceased giant to determine just how much of a dope addict he was and what kind of dope he used."

"*Dope* addict!" Penny said dazedly.

"Yes, I noticed that both arms had a lot of hypo scars, old and new. He was undoubtedly what you call a 'mainliner,' I believe, and by the looks of it had been for some time. It opens up quite a Pandora's box when you think about it."

"But how do you know about dope and such?"

"You're not the *only* one who watches crime shows, you know," Toby said frostily.

Penny was momentarily diverted by this unexpected insight. "But I thought you spent all your evenings drinking in the Lamb and Flag!"

"Even the Lamb and Flag has a television in the bar

these days," Toby said gloomily. "The noble old art of conversational communication of the saloon is now as dead as the dodo." He sighed. "In any case, I know quite a lot about it firsthand, because one of my better students got hooked a couple of years ago, and I got very involved helping him kick the habit."

Penny in turn sighed faintly. Toby was such an extraordinary creature. To hear him talk most of the time, you could easily believe that he regarded all students as a wild, savage and distinctly separate species from himself. However, occasionally he would let fall something like this, which indicated quite the opposite.

"I also convinced Hamit Bey," Toby droned on, "that we might be of some help with the people at the hotel; so I don't think we have to worry about imminent incarceration."

"I wouldn't bet on it," Penny said. "Hamit Bey strikes me as a thoroughly unpredictable character. I'll pin my faith on Bilger Kosay. He, at least, is friendly."

"I wouldn't put too much stock in that," Toby said stonily.

"Whyever not? He was most helpful to me."

"Why?"

"*Why?* Well, *I* don't know. Perhaps I remind him of his mother or something," Penny said heatedly.

"Highly unlikely," Toby sniffed. "Far more likely that it is the old police ploy of having a 'heavy' and a 'good guy,' so that the suspect, after a bad session with the heavy, tells all to the good guy." The Americanisms sounded extremely strange delivered in Toby's precise Oxford accent. He twinkled at her suddenly. "The fruits of television again, you see! Anyway, just don't be *too* open and trusting with Mr. Kosay, because I don't think he's. that trustworthy. Nor," he added thoughtfully, "does Hamit Bey, apparently. I wonder why?"

"Well, you stick to your policeman and I'll stick to mine," Penny said with some force. They had reached the hotel, and the thought of a nice, soft bed in a pleasantly cool bedroom suddenly overwhelmed her. "I'm all in," she said simply, "so if you are going to play detective, you'll have to do without me for a while. I've got to have a nap."

"Good idea. Try and get your subconscious working on what you remember about Washington Thompson," Toby said. "I may lie down myself. I have some heavy thinking to do about our *modus operandi*. See you at dinner, then."

"I really believe you're starting to enjoy this," Penny said accusingly.

He thought about that for a moment. "You know, I think you're right!" He chuckled and ambled off.

Penny was so ravenous when they came down to a late dinner that she was not prepared to listen to anything Toby had to say until she had polished off in succession a *yumurta ispanak*, a large order of *karisik isgara* with *yesil salata* on the side, and some hunks of the delicious local bread with goat cheese and was topping it off with an extra-sticky *baklava*. At last she waved a fork in his direction and said, "Oh, I've remembered about Washington Thompson."

Toby, who was a picky eater at the best of times, and particularly so when he was preoccupied, and who had been watching her gastronomic performance with silent amazement as he sipped his wine, raised an encouraging eyebrow.

"It *was* a dope scandal," Penny said. "He played for one of the big California teams—the Los Angeles Rams, I think—and several of the players got suspensions for taking 'uppers' before games. This was about two years ago, by the way. Most of them were reinstated eventually, but he was let go. Then he got arrested on a charge of possession, but I don't think he was convicted, for some reason. After that he just faded out of the football scene—and into the movies, I guess. Maybe he was a 'pusher,'" she added helpfully. "Did you come up with anything during your cogitations?"

"So far, only general principles," Toby replied. "Obviously, the first thing we've got to do is to get inside this magic circle." He jerked his head toward the few tables that still remained occupied. "I can put names on most of these, thanks to the manager, but so far that's all. However, just seeing them has given me food for thought." He leaned over and said very quietly, "You see the girl at the table by herself? She's Washington Thompson's widow. What do you make of her?"

Penny took a quick, cautious glance. "Black but not negroid."

He nodded. "That's what I thought, but what racial grouping would you put her in?"

Penny took another look. "Australoid, I'd say. Not Melanesian Australoid, either—their hair tends to be kinkier —but genuine Australian Abo, I'd hazard a guess."

Again he nodded agreement. "Now look at that other table over by the window. What would you say about those two?"

Penny obliged, and her eyes widened slightly. "Japanese, without a doubt—look at those teeth—and Plains Indian. Wow, what a magnificent creature *he* is!"

"So?" Toby prompted. "What racial groupings?"

Penny turned reluctantly away from her contemplation of the handsome hawklike profile of the Indian. "Specialized Mongoloid and generalized Mongoloid, of course. What *are* you getting at?"

"Because *in* this small group we have represented all the major racial groupings in the world today. Quite a coincidence. It is just an idea, mind you, but something you said about the missing body struck me. You were so surprised to see her dressed up like that, because she was such a perfect specimen of the Nordic type."

"Yes—well?"

"Until I find out what the picture is about, I can't go much further." Toby worried at his thoughts. "I know the title, which is a damn silly one—*The Travels of Telemachus*—and that's all. But here you have a Nordic cast as a Greek maiden, a Negro cast as a Roman gladiator, though *what* a Roman gladiator has to do with the son of Ulysses, God only knows! Now, just supposing that all the racial types represented here have equally bizarre castings, that the picture had some 'campy' racial angle?"

"You mean there's some nut who doesn't *like* this angle and is polishing them off in sequence?" Penny interposed. "It seems terribly far-fetched."

"I suppose it does," Toby said faintly, "but it wouldn't hurt to keep an especially close eye on Mrs. Thompson and our Mongoloid characters over there. In any case, that's just one possibility; the other, and possibly the more likely one, is the dope thing."

"My body didn't have hypo marks on it," Penny said firmly. "I couldn't have missed that, because she had such white skin the least mark would have shown."

"That doesn't mean she couldn't have been mixed up in it," Toby said testily. "We're not all that far from Afyon Karahissar and the center of the opium-growing region here in Bergama. Also, you remember that Scrowski Productions, according to that label you saw, has Marseilles as one of its centers—and *that* strikes me as odd. Paris, maybe, but Marseilles?"

"Hmm. I see what you're getting at," Penny said. "Did you see *The French Connection,* too?"

"I *never* go to the cinema," said Toby loftily. "A terrible waste of time!"

Penny chose to ignore him. "So you think they may be 'carriers' or something in the dope business? I suppose a film company would make a good cover, at that, come to think of it. An outfit like this moves about a lot, and with all the equipment they carry, customs men might get slapdash. Yes, that's quite a thought. What other bright ideas did you have?"

"Well, we've got these two lines of inquiry to start on, and I thought, once we'd found the key into this little circle, we could divide things up and you could concentrate on the women and I'd concentrate on the men."

"Why not let *me* concentrate on the men and you on the women," Penny said brightly but, at Toby's reproving glare, subsided muttering, "Just a joke. Incidentally, who or what was this female you were fleeing from this morning? You never got around to telling me about that."

Toby twitched convulsively, spilling some of his wine, "Oh, ye gods! I'd almost managed to forget her." He looked hauntedly around. "She isn't here, thank heavens, but she must be one of them. Wore the most *extraordinary* getup, a sort of Gypsy bandana around her head and a long, flowing robe of some sort, simply festooned with jewelry. She had the whole zodiac slung around her, I swear, together with sundry ankhs and *crux ansata, ad infinitum.*"

"What did she look like?" Penny demanded with interest.

"You couldn't tell under all the make-up. Kohled eyelashes about an inch long and rather shrewd, beady black eyes embedded in a field of green malachite—"

"Eye shadow," Penny volunteered kindly. "Nowadays it's mascara and eye shadow, Toby. Kohl and malachite went out with ancient Egypt."

"She looked like something from ancient Egypt," Toby moaned, "straight out of a tomb!"

"Well, what did she want?"

"Me, I think," Toby said with horror. "She must have found out from the manager or someone that I was an archaeologist. Anyway, she seized me, quite literally, and said she was so glad to find me here, that her 'guide' had told her she would meet someone to whom she would mean much, and that she knew it was I! She said she could help me in my work, because she could remember all the details of at least six of her reincarnations, starting as a princess in ancient Egypt, that she had wonderful things to reveal to me, and when could we get together in private, away from the hostile vibrations of the outside world, so that our karmas could meld. Then she asked me if I was married." He shuddered and took a large gulp of wine.

"Poor Toby," Penny chuckled. "And then what happened?" She looked up to see Toby, his glass suspended in midair, looking fixedly over her shoulder, an odd expression of his face.

"What is it?" she hissed. "Did she just come in?"

He lowered the glass and shook his head slowly. "I think," he said carefully, "that our open sesame to the magic circle has just appeared. Unless I am very much mistaken, Joshua White just walked in."

"*The* Joshua White?" Penny murmured and turned to see a small, grizzled figure standing unsteadily in the doorway, as Toby, his face fixed in a cherubic grin, walked past her, hand outstretched, booming, "Why, Josh, what a delightful surprise. Remember me, Toby Glendower? And what happy chance brings you to Bergama?"

CHAPTER 4

Toby had detached Joshua White from his two companions
—very skillfully, Penny thought—and had brought him
over to the table. The two men who had come in with him
now hovered uncertainly in the middle of the room, gazing
somewhat forlornly after the small man. One was of in-
determinate age, small, slight, bespectacled and sandy-
haired; the other, young, almost baby-faced, tall, gangly
and with a pair of very striking blue eyes, painful in their
vulnerability. Disparate as the pair were, they both wore
the same deeply worried expression.

As the introductions were performed, a whiff of whisky-
laden breath gave Penny a clue as to the possible source of
their worry. If Joshua White wasn't already stoned, she
thought, he was well on the way to being so.

Snapping black eyes peered at her from under the bushy
gray brows. "Hmm, Dr. Spring . . ." As if to remind himself, Josh White rattled off some of the main areas of her
fieldwork and accomplishments, ending with "You wrote
that book on the position of women in pastoral societies,
didn't you? Read it. Didn't think much of it."

"Quite a lot of people didn't," Penny said dismally.

He seated himself and then grinned savagely at her,
tobacco-stained teeth showing through his heavy gray
beard. "Still, you made the right choice. Not like me."

Penny looked puzzled, so he enlarged, "I mean, you
went the right way across the Atlantic. An American at
Oxford—mind—your p's and q's and you're set for life,
eh? They don't throw you away because you get old." He
snorted and turned to Toby, who had been quietly sum-
moning up drinks. "I suppose you heard I had to leave my
university job at U.S.C. Too old, they said. Bah!"

Toby grunted noncommittally.

"But I showed them!" Again Josh grinned savagely.

"Making more now than I ever did as an archaeologist—
mug's game, that. Technical adviser, that's what I call
myself now. Technical adviser to any and all of Scrowski's
historical productions. They don't know it yet, but they
are going to help finance the dig of the site of the century."
He winked craftily. "And I bet you'd like to know where
that's going to be!"

"You're technical adviser to the—er—*Travels of Telemachus*?" Toby said carefully.

Josh White gave a sharp bark of laughter. "Yes. Lot of
bilge, of course, but I get my kicks making them get the
little details right. Drives 'em crazy! But"—he became
owlishly solemn all of a sudden—"all the same, it's not
like when we dug Tepe Gasa together, Toby. Now, *there*
was a dig." And he began to reminisce.

Penny listened abstractedly to the two men, Toby's deep
musical rumble intermingling with Josh's sharp, staccato
bark, which still carried an underlying stratum of Cock-
ney despite a heavy overlay of pseudo American. She ran
over what she knew about Josh White. He was one of the
last great, colorful characters of the "old school" of archaeologists, men like Woolley, Leakey and Wheeler, who
had become legends in their own time. But, while these
men had reaped fame and acclaim, the greater honors had
somehow eluded Joshua White. About him had always
hung a slightly shady aura, and she wrinkled her brows
in an effort to remember why this had been.

Women—that had been part of it, she knew. Josh had
been a great womanizer, and when he took his bitter and
very well publicized leave of England just after the
Second World War, there had been strong rumors that his
university had been more than relieved to see him go. Had
he been up to his old tricks in the States?

Although Penny was well aware of the New World's
"cult of youth," she knew equally well that in the rarefied
atmosphere of anthropology and its sister sciences, one
could also go on indefinitely in America, providing you
were eminent enough—*and* responsible.

Possibly it was women *and* drink. He was certainly
soaking it up now at a rapid enough rate. She glanced
across and caught Toby's eye. He raised one eyebrow and
gave a slight dismissive nod. Obviously, he wanted to get

down to brass tacks with Josh before the latter was too far gone in his cups, and her presence might be an inhibiting factor on any confidences.

She got up rather hastily and said, "I'm sure you two have a lot to talk about; so, if you'll excuse me, I'll just have a word with poor Mrs. Thompson." The men half rose, but Josh did not so much as check his stream of conversation as Toby gave her a quick, encouraging smirk before turning back to the older man.

With some hesitation, Penny went up to the table where the black girl was sitting gazing into a coffee cup. "Excuse me, Mrs. Thompson," Penny said a little breathlessly, "but I would like to offer my most sincere condolences on your tragic loss and to say that if there is anything I can do to help at this difficult time, I would be only too happy to do so. My name is Penelope Spring."

Opaque black eyes looked up at her. "Such as?" inquired the soft voice with a nasal Australian twang.

"Well—er—anything," Penny said lamely and hastily sat down. "Sometimes it is a help just to have another—er —older woman around at a time like this." She tried to look motherly. "Someone just to—well—talk to."

"Too right," the younger woman assented and looked at her with a level gaze.

"You're not American?" Penny said feebly.

"No. Pure Australian Abo, as you probably well know, Dr. Spring."

"You know who I am?" Penny was taken aback.

"Sure. I recognized you the minute you came in. Your picture is on the back of all your books, and I took anthropology at U.S.C." There was a glint of mockery in the dark eyes. "Suitable subject, don't you think? And if you're wondering what I was doing at U.S.C., I was there on an athletic scholarship." The dark lips parted in a slight grin, revealing startlingly white, even teeth. The girl shook her head slightly. "Not tennis this time—fencing and gymnastics. We Abos are coming on strong, aren't we?"

Penny refused to take this bait but carried on gamely. "And it was there you met your husband?"

"Oh, yes indeed. Washington Thompson, the superjock." Her tone was bitter. "Those were the good days, though." She sighed and fell silent.

"Have you any idea who may have done this terrible thing?" Penny asked hesitantly.

The girl jerked a chin around the room. "Take your pick. Any one of this fun-filled family wouldn't have been sorry to see him off. Washington's specialty was making enemies. Not that I think any of this crowd here murdered him; it's the one who *isn't* here who most probably did it. Anyway, that's what I've told the police. If they find her, they'll most likely have the right one."

"Her?" Penny prompted.

"Yes, Melody Martin—that bloody tramp! She'd gone through every other man in the company, our leading man included, but she was after Washington as well. It's hard to believe he wouldn't have obliged her, too, but maybe he had other things on his mind. Anyway, two can play at that game," she added obscurely, her glance smoldering across the room to where the hawk profile of the Indian bent toward his Oriental companion.

"Well, I'm very sorry for you and him, both," Penny said quietly.

"No need to be." The tone was vehement. "If I'd had to stay around this bloody lot much longer, I'd have probably pointed a bone at him myself."

"You also were involved in the movie?"

"In this two-bit outfit, we *all* are involved, both behind and in front of the cameras. Yes, I was in the film. Circe's daughter, complete with acrobatic dance, and wardrobe mistress as well."

"Isn't that a bit unusual?" Penny said tentatively.

"Not when you get a shoestring operator like Scrowski. Don't let the fancy fronts fool you—Scrowski always has an angle. His productions are cheap, and so is his hired help, for a variety of reasons. It's the way he operates."

"And this Melody Martin?"

"The blonde bombshell? One of Scrowski's ex-tarts. He's an old ram of the vintage Hollywood school. But how she wangled this role I don't know. Must have had something good on the old b. Anyway, Carla Vincent, who was originally cast as Telemachus's girlfriend—the female lead —was out on her can, and Melody was in before anyone knew what was going on."

A faint sinking feeling came over Penny. "And Melody Martin was cast as a Greek girl? What did she look like?"

"Blonde, peaches and cream, everything in the right place, a great pair of legs. Quite wrong for the part, of course, and rotten, rotten clean through. Though why she should empty three bullets into Washington and then split is beyond me. It would have been a lot easier for her to get the poor bastard canned."

Penny hesitated for a moment, then took the plunge. "I don't think Melody Martin could have killed your husband," she said quietly.

"Oh? Why not?" The tone was sharp.

"Because I found her body this morning," Penny said earnestly, "a good two hours before your husband was killed, so whoever did kill him, it wasn't she." She looked up and was faced by an inscrutable black mask. "Indeed?" The soft voice was sibilant. "How strange that the police made no mention of this to me!"

Penny was not about to launch into a lengthy explanation. Instead she said, "I assure you it is so, and it seems likely that the two deaths are connected. Have you any idea what the connection might be?"

The girl got up, and Penny noticed for the first time how small she was—a couple of inches shorter than her own diminutive height. *How on earth did they ever manage . . . ?* the vagrant thought flickered through her mind. She said quickly, "I hope I haven't upset you. I certainly did not mean to, but obviously it *is* important."

The eyes were now veiled. "No, I'm not upset," the soft voice assured her. "But if it wasn't Melody, then I don't know. I just don't know." And to Penny's sharpened senses there seemed an edge of fear to the whisper.

She threw a quick glance across at Toby and Josh White, who were still deep in their conversation. "I'll come with you." She got up quickly. "It has been quite a day, so I think I'll turn in early—that is, if you are sure there is nothing I can do to help you."

"Nothing—unless you happen to have the price of a fare back to Sydney on you." The quiet voice was cynical. "But I don't suppose they'd let me go, anyhow."

They walked silently to the door.

"Oh, Gale! Could I have a word with you?" The

splendid form of the Indian almost catapulted toward them in one lithe, pantherlike bound, and the brilliant, deep-set eyes swept curiously over Penny like the beam of a searchlight as he intercepted them.

Gale Thompson stopped and looked up at him with an enigmatic expression. "Sure, Wolf, what is it?"

He opened the door and motioned her out, but she stood firm and turned to Penny.

"Oh, Dr. Spring, I'd like you to meet Wolf Vincent, our chief cameraman and propman. Wolf, this is Dr. Spring, the anthropologist. She's living here." For an instant the girl's dark eyes held Penny's mild hazel ones, and there was an expression in them that Penny could not quite decipher. Warning, challenge, urgency? She wasn't sure.

The handsome head bowed briefly in acknowledgment, and then he took Gale's arm and guided her firmly away.

Penny moved to follow them but was stopped in her tracks by an arresting sight. Clanking toward her across the hall foyer with a purposeful lope came the tall figure of a woman whose turbaned head and multiple jewelry left no doubt as to her identity. Penny thought quickly. If the woman spotted Toby inside, she would undoubtedly pounce, and bang would go his tête-à-tête. Penny would have to head her off somehow.

She let out a convincing gasp of surprise and hastily rummaged in her shoulder bag, "Oh, when they told me *you* were here, I could scarcely believe it! I've always been such a fan of yours! I wonder—would it be too much to ask—could I have your autograph? I'd be *so* grateful!"

The figure halted in midlope, and the dark, beady eyes opened wider in surprise. "But of course," she announced in a deep contralto and extended an imperious hand. "I am ever at the command of my public."

As the woman scribbled the name "Gloria de Witt" in a large, flamboyant style, Penny hastily searched her mind for any recollection of her. She was terrified that the apparition would next demand which of her pictures Penny preferred, and Penny could not even dimly remember having seen the masklike, painted face before her.

Toby's description hadn't been too sound, she reflected, since his "Gypsy bandana" was definitely an Indian-style turban. Then she noticed that the festooned jewelry consisted now of Indian swastikas, stylized pipal trees, a Buddhist fertility horn, and assorted Siva and Kali figurines; so she concluded that the remarkable Gloria de Witt had undergone a transformation of both costume and philosophy since the morning.

"Oh, thank you, thank you *so* much," she gushed as Gloria de Witt graciously handed her back the scrap of paper. To her vast relief, the inevitable question when it came was a rhetorical one. "No doubt you saw me in *The Flaming Vessel*," Gloria de Witt trumpeted.

"Oh, yes, yes indeed," Penny agreed. "Your finest role!"

"Hmm. Not my finest, perhaps," the tone was complacent. "I have always thought my role in *The Daughters of Sin* had more depth to it, though the movie as a movie was not such a strong vehicle."

God, she must date to the early thirties, or even before. She must be as old as the hills! Penny thought. *But, whatever I do, I've simply got to keep her talking.* "And now you're in *The Travels of Telemachus?*" she said hastily. "I shall so look forward to that, particularly now that I've met you."

"Alas, yes." Gloria de Witt put a scrawny, beringed hand over her heart and closed her eyes as if in pain. "Like all modern movies, a thing not to be talked of in the same breath as the *real* cinema of former days, but with this modern cult of bodies and general ugliness, an actress must bow before the storm and take what the Fates bring upon her." She sighed heavily. "Our destiny, after all, is writ *above.*"

"Oh, yes, how true!" Penny said eagerly, happy to be able to get off the dangerous quicksands of moviedom. "My colleague was telling me of the most interesting conversation he had with you this morning, and I would so like to discuss some of these things with you—er—astrology and so forth."

The small black eyes opened, bright and hard with suspicion, "Dr. Glendower is your colleague? You work with him?" Gloria de Witt queried sharply. Penny nodded. "And you are . . . ?" Gloria demanded.

"Penelope Spring. *Mrs.* Spring."

"You are also an archaeologist?" The tone was deeply suspicious.

"No, we merely teach at the same university, but in different fields," Penny assured her.

Gloria thawed a little. "A most interesting man," she confided. "I vibrated to his aura immediately. He has an incredible deep-blue one. I am a Scorpio, of course, the most psychic of the signs, so I *know* about people. He is a Capricorn."

"Oh, really? I'm afraid I don't know him that well," Penny lied cheerfully.

Gloria looked more kindly upon her. "You, of course, are a Cancer. I knew it the instant you spoke."

"How *clever* of you," Penny said. She was, in fact, a very solid Taurus. "I wonder, would you do me the honor of perhaps taking a walk with me? It is such a beautiful evening. And perhaps you would join me for a coffee at one of those delightfully quaint alfresco coffeehouses they have here."

Gloria de Witt regarded her dubiously. "I was looking for Dr. Glendower. Perhaps some other time . . . ?"

"Oh, he met an old colleague of his, Joshua White, whom you must know, of course. I believe they've gone off somewhere together," Penny volunteered.

An expression of distaste came over Gloria's face, and she let out a disgusted snort, "Joshua White! That *evil* man! An old soul—almost as old as my own—but evil. I trust Dr. Glendower will not suffer from his company. The man is *tainted!*"

"Er, yes, well, I think they did some digging together in the old days," Penny said hastily, "so they had some things to talk over. Won't you join me, then?"

Gloria de Witt unbent. "In that case I shall be happy to accompany you," she boomed.

Ten minutes later saw them installed at a rickety wooden table, the cynosure of the *lokanta*'s only other occupants, a small crowd of solidly staring Turkish men. Penny was too elated by the success of her diversionary tactic to be embarrased and cheerfully ordered two Turkish coffees from the popeyed waiter.

Gloria de Witt held up a restraining hand. "I think I'll have a double raki as well," she intoned. When the color-less liquid arrived, she expertly tipped it into the accompanying glass of water, watched with satisfaction as it milkily opalesced, and took a huge gulp before settling back with a rattle of chains into her chair. She looked expectantly at Penny, who was wondering what avenue of Gloria de Witt's labyrinthine ego might be the least exhausting to explore.

"And what part do you play in *The Travels of Telemachus*?" she asked finally.

A slightly pained expression came over Gloria's face. "Penelope."

"Yes?" Penny answered.

"*Penelope*—Telemachus's mother."

"Oh, I see. And does the part give you *scope*?" Penny hoped she was getting the phraseology right.

"It's a silly part in a very silly film," Gloria said unexpectedly. "A time fantasy, my eye! The original script wasn't too bad, but what they've done with it!"

Penny felt she hadn't got off to a very good start. She tried again. "Will this terrible tragedy today affect the movie very much?" she inquired tentatively.

Gloria dismissed Washington Thompson's murder with a derisive snort. "Not much, no. But it was just asking for trouble bringing in all these inferior races. When you get blacks and chinks around, there's always trouble. It was a ridiculous idea from the start, and I told Hyman so. But, of course, he wouldn't listen."

Penny started to bristle but thought better of it. Instead she said, "Hyman?"

"Hyman Scrowski." Gloria looked mildly shocked at the query. "The producer, you know. He and I are very old friends. In fact"—she drooped her baggy eyelids demurely—"there was a time when we were more than friends. He still knows the worth of good acting, though, which is why I agreed to play in this thing. As I told him, he'll need all the help he can get, with all the delays and mixups there have been." Then, half to herself, she said, "He should have been here by now. Heaven *knows* where he's got to. That will mean another delay, I suppose."

"It has been delayed before."

"Yes. They started to shoot with Carla Mann, or rather Carla Vincent, as she likes to be called, in the lead role opposite Brett Russell, but she wasn't right for the part;

so they started all over with Melody Martin, and then everything else got changed around."

"Carla Vincent? Is she Wolf Vincent's wife?" Penny asked with interest.

The old actress again sniffed expressively. "Well, that's the way she likes people to think of her. But, as far as I know, they've never made it legal, nor, if Wolf has any say in it, are they ever likely to."

"She must have been quite upset to lose the starring role to Melody Martin," Penny murmured.

"Flaming mad," Gloria said with considerable satisfaction. "So was Wolf, for that matter, even though he'd had a little thing going with Melody on the side at one time."

"I gather she wasn't very popular all round."

Gloria looked at her surprised. "Who told you that? Not one of the men, I warrant! Oh, there's nothing wrong with Melody—most of the women can't stand her because she's got more on the ball than they have. Personally, I think she's worth all of them rolled into one. She's a good little actress and has the looks to go with it. When she is on camera, the thing comes to life a bit; even Brett Russell perks up and gives a passable imitation of himself twenty years ago, instead of the middle-aged has-been he seemed at the beginning. Even Angus McLean has begun to get enthusiastic about it."

It was Penny's turn to be surprised. "Not *the* Angus McLean? The man who won all those Academy Awards back in the forties?"

Gloria nodded. "Yes, that's right. He's our director." There was an edge of reserve in her voice.

It was on the tip of Penny's tongue to say, "But I thought he was dead," but she wisely refrained and said instead, "I wouldn't have thought this kind of thing was his style. Wasn't he one of the first 'super-realists'?"

Gloria seemed to draw into herself; her answer was almost brusque. "He's lucky to be working at all. Most of the producers won't touch him with a barge pole, after the things that came out about him at the un-American activities purge they had sometime back. Even Hyman only dares employ him on the things he produces in Europe."

"Goodness!" Penny muttered faintly as another whole new vista of possibilities opened up in her mind.

Gloria was looking at her fixedly. "Who told you about Melody Martin?" she demanded again.

"Oh, Mrs. Thompson mentioned there had been some kind of trouble," Penny said vaguely.

"Oh, *her!* She'd say anything to start a fight. As I said, where there are blacks, there's always trouble," Gloria snorted contemptuously and got up jangling. "The night air is becoming too cool for me. I have to guard my voice, you know." She placed a hand against the cordlike tendons of her skinny neck. "I must get back to the hotel." All of a sudden she seemed to be in a hurry.

Penny got up, too. "Well, I've very much enjoyed our talk. Since we are both likely to be here for a while, I hope we can get together again."

Gloria de Witt inclined her head graciously but said nothing, and they walked in silence back to the hotel. An anxious glance at the dining room through the wide-open doors assured Penny that it was now completely vacant. Either Toby had finished his tête-à-tête or had carted Josh off to continue their drinking elsewhere.

She turned in relief to the tall figure standing quietly in the dimly lit foyer. "Thank you again, Miss de Witt. I hadn't realized how late it is, so I'll bid you good night."

The old woman took a pace toward her and leaned down, bringing her face close to Penny's. "Do you believe in destiny?" she hissed.

Penny recoiled. The aging actress had been talking so normally that this reversion to eccentricity came as a shock. "Well—er—up to a point," she stammered.

"Then, mark my words well," the old woman whispered. "Death has not finished his harvest here, not by a long shot. What happened today was just the beginning. There will be rainbows, but no pot of gold." And with that she turned and glided up the stairway, leaving Penny staring in dazed amazement after her.

CHAPTER 5

Penny was aroused from sleep by a light but persistent tapping on her bedroom door. She had been dreaming that she was racing up and down the aisles of the great Greek theater, attempting to catch a multitude of rainbow-colored butterflies, but whenever she stretched out her hand to capture one, they would fade away and become baby rainbows that retreated from her as she chased them. It had been a most exhausting dream; consequently she felt quite drained as she lay watching the bright sunbeams streaming in through the shutters, making bars of gold upon the tiled floor.

The knocking continued, and she realized a voice was calling her name softly. Muttering a little, she heaved herself out of bed, shrugged on a bathrobe and opened the door a cautious crack. The expectant eye of Bilger Kosay peered eagerly in at her. *"Bayan* Spring," he whispered, "I wonder if you would come with me now. I need your help."

Penny glanced at her watch and saw with mild horror that it was only seven o'clock. "I'm not up yet," she said crossly. "I haven't even had a cup of coffee. Can't it wait, whatever it is?"

"No, please, we should go now," Bilger persisted. "I'll explain why later, and we can get coffee for you on the way. Please, it is quite important!"

Penny grunted. "All right," she said ungraciously and closed the door in his face. She splashed some water on her face, gave her teeth a desultory scrub, threw on a pair of slacks and a sweater and brought some sort of order to her tousled hair; then she stumped back to the door and barked through it, "You still there? Where are we going, and what should I bring?"

"Nothing—just yourself."

She opened it to find Bilger gazing anxiously at her. "I'd better leave a note for Dr. Glendower," she said. "Where are we going?"

"That won't be necessary. We won't be gone long," Bilger said quickly. He turned and walked rapidly away from her. Penny followed, grumbling all the way to the waiting jeep. Even two cups of coffee did not restore her temper, and she sat huddled in a sulky heap as the jeep sped toward the ancient city on the hill.

"What's all this about?" she asked suspiciously when he drew up before the theater. "And why did we have to come at this ghastly hour?"

"I'll tell you, but first let's get inside, and we'll go to where you were sitting yesterday," Bilger said, urging her into the darkness of the tunnel.

"Well?" she challenged when they were sitting side by side, gazing at the same peaceful scene of the day before.

Bilger turned to her and said earnestly, "Hamit Bey is still unconvinced by your story, but *I* believe you. He has made it plain that he does not want anything done on this aspect of the case in working hours, but that doesn't mean I can't act in my own time. I don't have to be at the office before nine; so I thought you and I would go over the events of yesterday on the spot and see if we can come up with something new—maybe even locate the body."

Penny looked at him, popeyed, "But you've already searched this place and the amphitheater. Your men found nothing."

"I know"—he nodded impatiently—"but just listen to this outline and see what you make of it. One, the body was here on the stage at ten-thirty A.M. and yet had disappeared by the time we all got back here just after noon. Two, the shots that killed Washington Thompson in the amphitheater were fired, according to Dr. Glendower, at twelve-thirty-five P.M., and we found no trace of the girl's body there, either. Three, it is approximately two kilometers across country from here to the amphitheater, and about three and a half if you go by road. Four, according to your description, the girl was about five-foot-five in height and weighed about fifty-five kilos. Five, you heard no sound of a car—"

"Which doesn't mean that there wasn't one," Penny said quickly. "I'm not sure I'd have heard it if it was parked down the hill, and, anyway, I wasn't listening for one. Have you looked for tracks?"

"Yes, but it is much too dry. Even on the dirt the wind covers tracks in a matter of an hour or so," he muttered impatiently. "But what does all this suggest to you?"

"Nothing," Penny said promptly.

He looked at her with a pained expression. "Well, think about it! Suppose Thompson murdered the girl. He does so about ten A.M., presumably somewhere in the vicinity and then dumps the body on the stage—why, we don't know. Then he finds that someone has seen the body—namely, you. He doesn't go after you but instead decides to move the body. This must be just after you left at ten-thirty. Then, barely two hours later, he is shot by someone he meets in the amphitheater. He dies after saying one word, 'mammoth,' and has in his pocket a blue contact lens which may or may not have something to do with the missing girl."

"Who is presumably Melody Martin," Penny put in.

"Oh, you know about that, do you? Yes, she's missing, all right. Her bags got to the hotel, but she didn't." He paused briefly and shot a sharp glance at Penny before continuing, "Now, granted Thompson was a big, strong man, but Melody Martin was fairly tall and fifty-five kilos of dead weight; so she was no light load to carry easily for any distance."

"So you think he hid the body not in the theater itself but somewhere close by," Penny said, "and then went off to keep a rendezvous with his murderer?"

"It's a possibility, and a likely one," Bilger agreed. "And the most likely place?"

Penny thought briefly. "Somewhere in the temple ruins on the hill above?"

Bilger nodded enthusiastically. "Yes, and I even think he left us a clue. I think we should look for something with an elephant on it."

"An elephant isn't a mammoth," Penny said practically. "If he meant elephant, why didn't he say so?"

"Who knows what goes on in the mind of a dying

man?" Bilger said airily. "Anyway, it gives us a starting point. Shall we go?"

Penny got up slowly. "There's something that puzzles me about Thompson," she said thoughtfully. "Why, if he was the murderer and he saw me find the body, didn't he come after *me?* He could easily have caught me. Even when he waved that sword, it wasn't threatening so much as—well—theatrical."

Bilger nodded, "That thought occurred to me, too, and it suggests some other possibilities. For a murderer, he certainly did not act very homicidal, although, after he dumped the body on the stage, he may belatedly have seen you sitting up there and was on his way up to take care of and as you were coming down."

"Then, why didn't he finish the job?" Penny demanded. "He could have caught up with me before I even got out of the theater."

"The autopsy showed he was a drug addict, just as Dr. Glendower suspected; so maybe he was 'high' and not thinking straight—hence the odd dumping place for the body."

"Or possibly he *wasn't* the murderer," Penny murmured, "but knew who was and that's why he was killed."

"Again it is possible," Bilger said abruptly, "but there are several things about that I don't like; so why don't we just act on my present assumption and start looking for the body?"

An energetic hour and a half later found them both sitting on a stone sarcophagus, hot, flustered and completely frustrated. They had combed the ruins of the Great Altar, the Temple of Athene and the lesser appendages for any signs of elephants, mammoths or evidence of recent digging and had come up empty-handed.

"I was so certain we'd find it," Bilger said despondently.

Penny gave a weary sigh. "You took the wrong person along. I'm no expert in these things, but Toby could have told you like a shot if anything had been disturbed. In any case, this isn't the only place that's possible; the murderer may have taken her down the hill, not up. Why don't you bring Dr. Glendower here and let him help you?"

Bilger did not seem to take kindly to the idea. "We'll keep this to ourselves for the moment," he said shortly.

"Your friend is a friend of Hamit Bey, who is no friend of mine."

"Speaking of Hamit Bey, if you have to check in at nine, you're already late," Penny said mildly.

Bilger groaned and rubbed another dirt streak across his face, "Well, I suppose we'd better give it up for today."

On the way back to town, Penny asked, "Why didn't you think much of my idea about Thompson not being the murderer?"

"Oh, lots of reasons"—Bilger shrugged—"though I do think he may have had an accomplice, either witting or unwitting. It's still too early to say anything definite, but the way I see it, he and the girl may have been driven up to the theater in their theatricial getup by a third party who then took off—call him or her X. Thompson murdered the girl, hid the body and then went off across country to the amphitheater, where he met X, who then shot him either *because* he'd murdered the girl or because he'd bungled it or because that had been X's intention all along." He gave another big sigh, "There's so much we don't know."

"Well, it's early days yet," Penny said comfortingly.

Toby was standing on the doorstep of the hotel, looking extremely cross, as they drew up. He watched suspiciously as Penny scrambled out of the jeep and waved an encouraging farewell at Bilger. "Where on earth have you been?" he rumbled peevishly. "You had me worried. Come along. I've got a lot to tell you." He started to propel her along the street.

"Wait!" Penny wailed, "I haven't had my breakfast yet."

"You can have an early lunch," Toby said firmly. "I've got to talk to you where we won't be overheard."

Five minutes later found Penny seated glumly across the table from him at a tiny *lokanta*. "You know, I'm getting remarkably sick of Turkish coffee," she said plaintively. "It simply isn't very sustaining."

"Then, have tea instead," Toby replied unsympathetically. "I looked all over for you last night. Where did you disappear to?"

"I was keeping Gloria de Witt out of your hair," Penny snapped.

"Who?"

"Your ancient Egyptian friend."

"Oh, no!" he groaned. "She's quite mad, I suppose."

Penny looked thoughtful, took a sip of the sickly-sweet, lukewarm tea, shuddered and said, "No, I don't think so. In fact, I can't quite make her out or what she's up to. She comes on strong as a weirdo; then suddenly she's as normal as you please and quite shrewd. And then, bingo, she's back in the weirdo bit. She may be a schizo, of course, or she may have method in her madness, or she may just be a very good actress; but she was interesting—very. However, first things first. Since you are obviously bursting to tell me all, carry on."

Toby drew out a black leather notebook from his breast pocket and began to leaf through it. "Yes, I've garnered quite a harvest. My session with Josh was very rewarding, but let me give you the general picture before going into the details." He slapped various pockets and began bringing out sundry folded bits of paper. "First of all, we don't have such a long list of suspects as I feared. Not all the location crew are here; so the only ones we really have to concentrate on are the ones who were in Bergama between ten o'clock yesterday morning, when presumably your murder occurred, and twelve-thirty-five, when mine did." He sucked noisily on his pipe and handed her one of the folded sheets.

She read in his neat script:

> Brett Russell—lead actor (Am.)
> Angus McLean—director (Scot.)
> Joshua White—historical adviser (Eng.)
> Andrew Dale—assistant director & historical adviser (Am.) (dogsbody)
> Sensota Yamura—art director (Hawaiian-Jap. origin)
> Wolf Vincent—cameraman & prop. director (Sioux Indian)
> Carla Vincent—actress & asst. wardrobe mistress (Am.)
> Josephine Kleindienst—actress & treasurer (Am.)
> Gale Thompson—actress & wardrobe mistress (Aust. Abo.)
> Washington Thompson—actor & asst. prop. (Am.) (DECEASED)

Melody Martin—lead actress (Am.)
(DITTO?)

"Who is Josephine Kleindienst?" Penny demanded.

"I strongly suspect she is your Gloria de Witt," Toby mused. "I thought there was an unholy gleam in Josh's eye when he gave me her name. Undoubtedly that must be her real name and she is none too proud of it."

"How about Scrowski?"

"The producer?"

"Yes. According to Gloria, he should have been here yesterday. In fact, he was supposed to arrive *ahead* of them, but there has been no sign of him."

"Well, no harm in adding him to the list, I suppose," Toby mumbled and made the addition.

"He sounds a perfectly revolting man," Penny said, "so if he is around, he should stand out like a sore thumb. I can just picture him—gross, florid, with mean little eyes and a lot of black, sleeked-down hair, probably reeking of cigar smoke, flashily dressed and *loud!*"

Toby looked at her with a slight grin. "You know, sometimes you sound like a *very* proper Bostonian."

"Well, after all, I *am* a Bostonian," Penny retorted with some heat. "I'm no prude, as you well know, but that man sounds like the very end."

"But, so far as we know now, not involved," Toby added. "So let's get on. You may be right about the mean little eyes, because, according to Josh, he is the world's greatest penny pincher, ably aided and abetted, I might say, by Gloria de Witt (née Kleindienst). Hence this rather odd setup. This skeleton crew was here ahead of the rest, who should be arriving in a few days' time, to get everything 'mocked up' for some retakes. Apparently these were some of the early scenes of the film that had to be redone because they changed both the story *and* the lead actress."

"Yes, I know about that. So they've all been here before?"

"Several months ago, it appears—with the exception of the Thompsons and Melody Martin."

"That's interesting."

"Yes, I thought so, too."

"I'm interested in what Josh had to say about Melody."

Toby shook his head. "All in good time. Let me get some other things out of the way first. To start with, the picture—which I must say sounds the biggest heap of balderdash I've ever heard—started off as a fairly straight historical mishmash, with modern sequences at the beginning and end. Something about Telemachus finding the girl of his dreams, losing her, finding her again—you know, the usual bilge—with a sort of running commentary narrated by his modern-day equivalent. This was the *original,* with Brett Russell as Telemachus and Carla Vincent as his Greek maiden. Then, suddenly, Melody Martin was in, Carla demoted to a minor role, and the whole slant changed. Telemachus goes on a journey through time in his quest for his one true love. Along the way he meets people of all the races who somehow aid him in his search and from whom he learns tolerance, brotherhood, etc., etc., ending up in modern times with the girl in his arms and presumably a halo around his wise little head."

"Hmm. Well, there's your racial angle, right enough," Penny said, "but I thought our Mongoloid friends were on the other side of the camera."

"Yamura and Vincent? They are. Those parts are played by a couple of bit players who aren't needed for the segments they were filming here."

"Isn't that typical of Hollywood," Penny said critically. "The best-looking man for miles around and they hide him behind a camera. What a waste!"

"In his line he's the best there is, according to Josh."

"I suppose he's here because of Carla. Otherwise, why would he waste his time on a third-rate production?"

Toby shook his head, "No. Because of Angus McLean. They move around as a kind of package deal. This outfit is stiff with them. Carla came with Vincent and was given the lead role. The Thompsons were brought in—although there were literally scores of more experienced Negro actors available—on both Scrowski's and McLean's insistence, because they, too, came as a package."

"Two for the price of one?"

"Almost. Mrs. Thompson has never acted before, but she looked good on the credits. Did you know she was a gold-medalist in fencing at the last Olympics?"

"Really!" Penny was impressed. "And where do the rest fit in?"

Toby unfolded several more bits of paper, momentarily studied them with his lips pursed around his pipe, then went on, "Well, to run them down in sequence, here's what I've got.

"Brett Russell *was* a big star as a young man—swash-buckling type, you know—but he's been on the slide for some time and was glad to get this. A great ladies' man and has four or five ex-wives who keep him broke. A nice enough chap, Josh says, but slightly dim-witted.

"Angus McLean—very famous, though I shocked Josh by never having heard of him. He was in some kind of bad trouble years ago, about which Josh was very evasive."

"I can tell you something about that," Penny interpolated.

"Oh, good! I have him down as 'to be further looked into.' I certainly wish we had a few reference books around here. It would save a lot of time. I think I'll work on Hamit Bey to let me off the hook as far as Izmir and see if the British consulate there has any. Even a *Who's Who* might help."

"We're not interested in people's pedigrees," Penny said testily. "We just want to find out if one of them is a murderer."

Toby looked at her with mild reproach. "And the more we know about them, the easier it should be."

"Well, I very much doubt whether a *Who's Who* would list homicidal tendencies," Penny grumbled.

Toby sighed and went on. "Josh? Well, we know about him. Andrew Dale—he's that young man who came in with Josh last night. His official title is assistant director, but I gather he is supposed to pitch in on absolutely anything that needs doing. Has a finger in every pie. Fantastically bright, but a bit unstable. Used to be Carla Vincent's boyfriend before she married Wolf Vincent."

"According to Gloria de Witt, they aren't married," Penny put in.

"Oh!" Toby looked disapproving. "Well, whether they are or not, Andrew Dale is out in the cold and takes it very hard.

"Sensota Yamura—a very inscrutable Oriental. Has a

reputation for being a gambler, but that's about all. One odd thing is that there does not seem any particular reason why he should be here, because all the retakes were to be exteriors.

"Wolf Vincent—very good at his job and very touchy. Big in the Indian rights movement back in the U.S. Very much a man's man, but irresistible to the ladies, much to Brett Russell's chagrin."

"I'm not a bit surprised," Penny muttered.

"Hmm. Like that, is it?" Toby said frostily. "I thought I detected a maudlin note in your voice every time his name comes up."

"And what about Carla Vincent?" Penny said diplomatically.

"Very beautiful girl. Has a Greek mother and therefore looked the part to a T, but not much of an actress, I gather. Idolizes Wolf and is terribly jealous, so tends to throw temperamental fits, particularly of late.

"Josephine Kleindienst, or Gloria de Wift—presumably you can fill me in more on her. Josh didn't say much, other than that she's a king-size bitch, hard as nails and out for number one twenty-four hours a day. Absolutely no love lost between those two. Scrowski trusts her, and the rest of them look on her as his spy.

"Then the Thompsons. He was well loathed. Threw his weight around, literally, and was highly unpredictable. Even McLean, who is normally long-suffering and patient, had trouble with him. Not much on her, except that she wasn't particularly happy and bitched the whole time about missing Australia. And finally Melody Martin—"

"Yes, I've been dying to hear about her," Penny said eagerly.

"You may be disappointed. Josh wasn't very enlightening. He said she was a first-rate gold digger and full of herself and that he thought she had probably put pressure on Scrowski to get this role. When I tried to get more out of him on that, he shut up like a clam and went off at a tangent."

"It's strange," Penny mused. "So far I've heard three views on Melody Martin, and they've all been completely different. According to Mrs. Thompson, she was a nymphomaniac. Gloria de Witt said she was a fine actress and had more to her than any of the rest of them here. And Josh has her as a gold digger with perhaps a little blackmail on the side. I wonder which of them is the truest picture. They can't all be right."

"I should think you could well discount Gloria de Witt's view. She seemed as mad as a hatter to me," Toby sniffed.

"Oh, no, I think you are quite wrong," Penny said quickly and proceeded to give him a rapid précis of her conversations of the previous evening.

"I see," said Toby at the end of it. "Very interesting. It certainly amplifies a lot of people's motives. You say Gloria de Witt was quite unbalanced when she talked about the racial angle?"

"If you ask me," Penny said stoutly, "we've a sight too many motives already and far too few facts. The most common motives for murder are sex, money and desire for power; so I don't see why we have to beat the bushes for a way-out one like race fanaticism or drugs. On the sex angle alone the Thompsons make prime suspects. He may have killed Melody Martin for it or because she was bugging *him* for it, and then Mrs. Thompson may have pumped bullets into him in a jealous rage. Or she could have killed them both for that matter. Even though she's so small, as an expert fencer she'd probably have the skill to have killed Melody. As far as money and ambition go, what about Carla Vincent? She lost her job because of Melody, and her husband had been playing around with her—"

"But why should she kill Thompson?" Toby interrupted.

"Because he knew she had done it; so she had to get rid of him, too." Rapidly she borrowed Bilger's theory and presented it as her own.

"You seem a bit hard on your own sex, but I grant you these are all possibilities," Toby said carefully. "And, by the way, what were you doing up at the theater with Bilger Kosay this morning?"

"Detecting."

"Detecting what?"

"Well, if you must know, we were looking for the body."

"That was most foolhardy," Toby said severely. "As I've said before, you should be extremely wary of Bilger

Kosay and certainly not go careening off into the country-side alone with him at ungodly hours without letting someone know about it."

"Why on earth should I be wary of him?" Penny said heatedly. "He's the police, he bailed me out of durance vile, he believes in me, and he has taken me into his confidence. Why shouldn't I trust him?"

"Haven't you wondered how he happens to be such a fluent English speaker?" Toby said with upraised eyebrows.

"Well, I suppose he's good at languages and may have done some training in the States—a lot of Turks have," Penny said defiantly. "You don't have a monopoly on speaking other languages perfectly, you know!"

Toby shook his head. "He speaks fluently because he has always been bilingual. His mother is an American—and what's more, an American actress."

"Oh! So?" Penny said weakly. She suddenly wished she had another cup of tea. She glanced around the *locanta,* but the proprietor wasn't in sight.

"I'm just saying that Bilger Kosay may not be as unconnected with this affair as you think. He had a certain amount to do with the company when it was here the last time; so he already knows some of the people. I imagine he didn't tell you that, did he?"

"But how do you know it?" Penny challenged.

"Because Hamit Bey told me, and Josh mentioned him again last night."

Penny decided it was time to change the subject. "How far do you think Josh White is trustworthy?"

Toby furrowed his brows. "Not very. Even in his cups Josh is a pretty wily character, and I have the feeling he was quite aware that I was pumping him."

"Is he a drunk?"

"No—far from it. In fact, in the old days he scarcely touched the stuff. Used to lecture *me* about it, come to think of it." He sounded pained.

"What exactly were his problems in England? I seem to recall there was some scandal about women."

Toby looked thoughtful. "Josh always has been a womanizer, but that wasn't it. You say we have too many motives already, but I can give you another. Josh really left because of some very hot water he got into about the sale of antiquities, and though he claims he had to leave U.S.C. because of his age, I heard through the grapevine that he was in similar trouble over a dig he did in Palestine for them. He may still be up to his old tricks, and, again, what better medium could he have for smuggling than the props of a company like this? But, as you say, what we need are facts, so"—he uncoiled himself from his chair—"I think I'll go and gather a few more."

"Where are you going?"

"To see Hamit Bey and find out about the Thompson autopsy."

"Don't say anything about this morning, will you?" Penny said quickly.

"All right," he assented grudgingly, "but don't go off like that again without telling me. What are you going to do now?"

"Go back to the hotel and have some breakfast. I'm starved," Penny said with enthusiasm.

Toby looked at his watch. "You've missed it."

"Oh, *no!*" she wailed. "When do they start lunch?"

"Not before one o'clock. But, never mind, they say starvation sharpens the thinking processes," Toby said unkindly and started to lope off.

"Wait!" Penny called after him. "I think the process has already started. Aren't *you* forgetting something that *I've* just remembered? Something rather important?"

Toby's knoblike head swiveled on its long stalk, his eyes popping with amazement. "I? Forget? What, for instance?"

"How long would you estimate it will take us to solve these murders at the present rate of progress?" Penny asked maddeningly.

"What a ridiculous question! How on earth should I know? As long as it needs, I suppose. After all, there's no mad rush for us to get back to Oxford. Term doesn't start for another two weeks, and if we miss the first week or so, we can make up the classes later. Jessup may shriek a bit, but let him! I've done it before with no ill effects. Why? Not afraid of our revered head professor, are you?"

"Well, Jessup is part of it," Penny said with dangerous mildness, "but there's someone rather more important with whom you have a prior engagement—in, as I now recall, just about ten days. You can't have forgotten *that*, surely?

"An engagement?" Toby's brow was furrowed. Then, slowly, consternation came into his face, he removed his pipe from his mouth, and his eyes filled with panic. "Good *Lord!* I'd been trying not to think of it."

"Now you're there," Penny said encouragingly. "As I recall, you're supposed to bow your knee before the queen and be duly dubbed Knight-Commander of the British Empire precisely eleven days from now."

"Good *Lord!*" Toby repeated. "That is a bit of a facer, isn't it? Well, I suppose if things drag on here, I'll just have to send regrets or something." He sounded vaguely hopeful.

"There's no use taking that line," Penny said sternly. "We've been all through this before, when you made such a fuss about accepting it in the first place. This is *not* the time to become your father's son, Tobias Glendower, and turn your back on the English crown." Toby winced at this low blow. "You know full well how furious Jessup was when they gave the knighthood to you rather than to him. Just think what mileage he'll make out of it if you don't turn up at the investiture because you happen to be mixed up in a couple of Turkish murders! You'll take years to live it down."

"I suppose so," Toby rumbled unhappily, pulling himself together with a visible effort. "Then, we'll just have to solve them in less than ten days; so the sooner we get to work, the better. I'm sure you'll think of something useful to do while I'm with Hamit Bey, particularly now that we're up against it." He gave her an encouraging nod and loped rapidly off.

"Not starving, I won't," murmured Penny.

A short while later she was gazing with considerable satisfaction and anticipation at the fruits of her labors: a bag of oranges, two large slabs of chocolate and a packet of rather sickly-looking French biscuits. She hurried off toward the improbable-looking facade of the so-called Egyptian Basilica, which shone deep red in the morning sun. *This should keep me going until lunch, and I can take my snack inside,* she told herself happily. *There won't be many tourists around, even if it is in downtown Ber-*

gama, and I can sight-see and eat at the same time. I've had quite enough detecting for one day.

She bustled through the ornate entrance and, spotting a suitably ruined pillar of the right height, made purposefully for it. As she came abreast of it, she became aware of a human tableau in the shadow of one of the side arches of the aisle. A man and woman stood in close embrace, the dark head of the woman buried in the chest of the young man. His arms were clasped around her shoulders, which were shaking with sobs. A pair of vivid blue eyes met Penny's over the dark head, and, with a muttered exclamation, Andrew Dale abruptly thrust his companion from him and strode past Penny, his face set and white, his blue eyes blazing.

The girl turned and stared wide-eyed at Penny. Her face was classically beautiful in the Grecian style, but it was marred at the moment by an unmistakably blackened eye. Penny had just time to note that the body was not quite in keeping with the perfection of the face before the girl let out another loud sob, then, turning quickly on her heel, plunged out of sight into the darkness. Penny could hear the clatter of her heels as she fled out of the temple in a direction opposite to that taken by Andrew Dale.

Penny carefully seated herself on the pillar and arranged her array of foodstuffs. *Well!* she thought as she bit into the chocolate. *So now I've seen Carla Vincent! I wonder who gave her that black eye—and why?*

CHAPTER 6

"Do you think they can be lovers?" demanded Hamit Bey and then shook his head and answered his own question. "No! It is impossible to imagine: she is too old and too much like a monkey."

"But a very amiable monkey," Bilger put in. He had argued so much with his chief in the past two days that he did not feel inclined to take up the cudgels again on an irrelevant issue. On the other hand, he had taken quite a fancy to Penny and felt that the least he could do was to put in a kind word for her.

This topic of conversation had long been one of the favorite subjects of speculation among the anthropological and archaeological students of Oxford University, and, as befitted that ancient seat of learning, the thinkers presented the widest spectrum of views, ranging all the way from scholastic sublimation and platonic love to more basic and earthly varieties. The principals in the matter were quite unconscious of the interest their inseparability aroused and never gave their close relationship a passing thought. It was a thing they took for granted, though if they were to be told they had to spend twenty-four hours a day together, they would take a hasty and horrified departure in opposite directions for destinations unknown. There were areas of both their lives that were strictly private and jealously guarded as such, but in the main they were inseparable because they found one another endlessly interesting, stimulating and entertaining. So, if that be love, they were lovers.

"Bergama would seem an unlikely place for a love affair," the chief of police worried on. "What do you suppose their real reason for coming here could be?"

Bilger tried to check his rising impatience. "I think it is just as they said—part of a tour to see old sites, that is all."

"And his offer to help—I do not understand that, either," Hamit Bey muttered suspiciously. "Yet when I checked with Ankara, I met with a sharp rebuff and was told to show him every courtesy and assistance. I do not understand it."

There's a hell of a lot you don't understand, the young man thought fretfully and started as the door opened and a uniformed constable ushered in the round-shouldered subject of their speculations.

Toby was wearing his most innocently cherubic expression and, as was his wont when he wanted something, moved with almost snaillike deliberation. Luckily Hamit Bey found this soothing. After the usual flowery greeting, Toby arranged himself slowly in the offered chair and unhurriedly stuffed and lit his pipe. After that he carefully searched through his pockets and began to pile a small sheaf of papers, one by one, on the desk. Then he raised guileless blue eyes to Hamit Bey and rumbled, "I have brought you the fruits of my labors, as promised. Would you like me to go over them now?"

Hamit gave him an understanding look and turned to Bilger, whom this display of slow motion had left almost dancing with impatience. "I want you to take the statements about the stabbing in the market yesterday and, when you've done that, see if there is anything in from Istanbul yet about Scrowski and that other matter."

Bilger glowered and left.

"Now," said Toby through a reflective puff of smoke, "I have prepared a précis in Turkish, but I am afraid my grammar is not all that it should be; so if you have any questions . . ."

He fell silent as Hamit began to read a very abbreviated version of what Toby had told to Penny. Finally Hamit said, "You have done excellently to find out so much in so little time. How did you manage it?"

"Kismet," Toby said with a grin. "I found that an ex-colleague of mine, Joshua White, is on the technical staff of this picture. The information comes from him."

"And is this—er—Joshua White to be trusted?"

"Not entirely," Toby said suavely. "Like yourself, Hamit Bey, I am suspicious of anyone who volunteers a lot of information for no specific reason. But I must add that a lot of this had to be dragged out of him."

He looked at Hamit with a twinkle in his eyes, and the other responded with a sudden grin and a brisk nod. "Excellent. I see we understand one another, *Bay* Glendower. And what can I do for you?"

Toby continued to regard him lazily through a halo of smoke. "Well, if it is not too much trouble, I would be most interested in the autopsy report on Washington Thompson."

Hamit nodded. Drawing out a sheet of paper from the folder on his desk, he began to skim through it. "You were right in thinking that Washington Thompson was a dope addict. According to the doctor, he probably has been on the hard stuff about a year: there was a considerable amount of kidney degeneration and a certain amount of muscular atrophy, and the blood test showed he had had a shot of heroin a few hours prior to his murder."

"Heroin, eh?" Toby murmured.

"As to the cause of death," Hamit read on, "three bullets from a thirty-eight caliber revolver, possibly of American make. We have to check with Ankara on that, because we just don't have the facilities here. It was not fired at close range, because there were no powder marks. None of the bullets hit vital spots, which was why he was still alive when you reached him. That was also why you did not see the murderer, who probably fired from the shelter of the amphitheater arcade somewhere."

"Then, you no longer consider me a suspect?" Toby queried.

Hamit smiled grimly at him. "Let us say that it is still a possibility, but one that would greatly surprise me, since you passed the paraffin test with flying colors. In any case, you were not thinking of going anywhere, were you, *Bay* Glendower?"

"No, the thought had not even crossed my mind," Toby agreed cheerfully, then sobered. "Could he have got the heroin from a local supplier in Bergama?"

Hamit Bey shook his head. "I very much doubt it. About the only center of action in that area was Izmir, but even that well is dry at the moment. There was a very big drug roundup about four months ago; all the Turks involved are now in jail, and Interpol got most of the others. A lot of chains got broken." He reflected a moment. "Raw opium is fairly easy to come by in Turkey—after all, they even put a little in some of our cigarettes and beer—but refined heroin? That's a lot harder to get hold of. Most of the refining gets done in France or Italy, and then it is distributed to world markets."

"Marseilles and Rome," Toby murmured absently.

Hamit threw him a sharp glance. "Among others."

"Presumably the drug syndicates will be making efforts to open up their channels of supply again."

"Undoubtedly."

"And Scrowski Productions first came to this area about three months ago?"

"That fact had not escaped me."

"Did you realize that Washington Thompson and his wife and the missing Miss Martin were not part of the original group?" Toby indicated one of the sheets of paper with his pipestem.

Hamit drew it to him and perused it with a frown. "So I see. You are hinting that perhaps they had stumbled on something and so were removed?"

"It's a possibility," Toby agreed. "And am I to assume from your last remark that you have come to accept Dr. Spring's account of Miss Martin's murder?"

"It is beginning to look as if something has happened to her," Hamit said grudgingly. "No trace of her has so far been found."

"I presume you are already doing so, but, under the circumstances, it would do to keep an eye on Mrs. Thompson's welfare—at least until the drug possibility is clarified one way or another."

"That will be taken care of." Hamit Bey fell silent for a moment, as if debating something; then he said slowly, "We have examined Miss Martin's effects at the hotel. In the main, they were innocent enough—clothes, cosmetics, and so on—but there were one or two items of interest. These effects consisted of a large suitcase and a traveling case—no sign of her purse—and the traveling case had a false bottom." He opened his desk drawer and drew out something. "In the hidden compartment were these." He held up a key ring from which dangled three keys. "These are all safe-deposit-box keys. One is to a box in Istanbul—this we are tracing now. Another is American-made and presumably is to a safe-deposit box in the States somewhere. The third is French. One wonders what a lady of Miss Martin's young years and comparatively humble circumstances would need so many safe-deposit boxes for.

"There was also this." "This" was an ordinary pad of airmail paper, which he handed to Toby.

Opening it, Toby found an unfinished letter bearing the date of three days before and written in a sprawling feminine hand. It read, "Hi, Hy! Hope to see you *alone* before you get back to the Mad Mob. There's a lot we've got to talk about, if you know what I mean! Also, there's something going on that I think you should know about. You told me to keep my pearly little ears open, and, boy, have I! It looks as if you are being crossed but *good* . . ." And at that point the letter broke off.

"Judging by where it was found, this was something she wanted to keep strictly to herself. Presumably it was meant for Hyman Scrowski, concerning whose whereabouts there seems to be a considerable conflict of opinion among the group at the hotel. According to *Bayan* de Witt he was supposed to be here ahead of them; according to *Bay* McLean he should have arrived with them; and according to *Bay* Vincent he was not planning to get here until everything was set up and the shooting begun. None of them seems to know where he is, and so far we, too, have failed to locate him. He certainly does not appear to be in Turkey, at least not legally."

"The fact that she never completed this letter seems to indicate that she believed he was on his way," murmured Toby. "A thousand pities from our point of view, since, beyond the fact that *something* was going on in the company which was not in accord with Mr. Scrowski's interests, it tells us absolutely nothing. However, I'll keep my ears open and try to discover what that something might be."

"You are concerning yourself very actively in this matter," Hamit Bey said with sharp suspicion again in his voice.

"Come now, Hamit Bey," Toby said amiably. "Surely it must be obvious to you that my main concern is to see this matter cleared up sufficiently so that Dr. Spring and I might continue on our interrupted vacation! We are innocent bystanders who, most unfortunately from our point of view, have become key witnesses in two murders; and, naturally, both she and I are most anxious to do everything we can to help." He thought it unwise at this juncture to mention the fact that it was imperative for them to return to England within ten days. In the first place, he was sure that it would seem to the readily suspicious chief like an excuse to leave the scene, and while the veracity of his story could be easily checked, he was overly sensitive to the fact that Hamit might construe this as an effort to put pressure on him to let them go. If need be, he would bring up the subject of the knighthood later, but for the moment . . . "Yes, we are indeed anxious to help clear this matter up," he repeated.

"Anxious" was the key word for Penny at that precise moment. After a brisk walk to shake down her snack, she had returned to the hotel and installed herself in the tiny and totally deserted lounge, whose stuffiness indicated it was seldom, if ever, used. She was scribbling a hasty letter to Alexander and wondering vaguely why the lounge should smell so overpoweringly of drains, even though she had thrown wide all the windows, when two voices caught her attention. The couple were obviously walking along the side of the hotel, oblivious to all but their own heated argument.

"Not another penny," Gloria de Witt was saying vehemently. "This has gone quite far enough. I warned you, Sensota, and so has Hyman. If you haven't got enough sense to heed our warning, tough!"

Strain as she might, Penny could not hear the Japanese art director's reply, although by his tone he was both angry and anxious.

"No!" said Gloria again. "After what has happened, I will do nothing until Hyman gets here—*nothing*, you understand! And threats won't help you anymore. . . ."

They passed out of earshot. A slight sound behind her made Penny jump, and she looked around to see Andrew Dale looking curiously at her from the doorway. He came in and closed the door firmly behind him, his movements tense, a stricken expression in his vivid eyes. "I'd like to

have a private word with you, Dr. Spring." His voice
wavered a little with nervousness.

"Why, certainly." She tried to smile reassuringly. "Come
and sit down. I was just writing a letter to my son. He's
just about your age; he's in his second year of medical
school at Johns Hopkins."

Andrew seated himself gingerly in one of the hard
and bilious-colored plastic lounge chairs and watched her
with a wary, guarded expression to which she was no
stranger. It seemed to her that every friend Alex ever
brought home had looked at her with that same look, as
if she were some unknown and dangerous species far
removed from their own. It reminded her of the look
strange dogs give you when they are unsure whether to
bare their teeth and bark or to wag their tails. She had
often been tempted to try the same remedy, namely, to hold
out her hand to be sniffed and declared friendly. If per-
fected, it would be a fairly simple device for bridging the
generation gap, she reflected wryly.

Now, however, she continued to smile silent encourage-
ment while Andrew gathered his courage to speak. Suddenly he burst out, "I wanted you to know that what you
saw in the Egyptian Basilica this morning has nothing to
do with the murder; so I would be most grateful if you
would not mention it to anyone—not even your friend."

Penny raised her eyebrows. "All I saw was a young man
comforting a young woman who needed it badly. Why
should I mention such an obviously private thing to anyone, Mr. Dale?"

"Well—er," he gulped, "I just thought I'd mention it
because—er—it might be misconstrued. I mean, Carla—I
mean Mrs. Vincent—well, it didn't mean anything . . ." he
trailed off.

"You can rest assured I shall say nothing of it to anyone," Penny said. "As far as I am concerned, it never
even happened."

He looked relieved, so she seized her opportunity and
went on. "I understand you are assistant director for this
movie. That must mean you are very good at your job, to
be working with someone like Angus McLean."

He seemed pleased with the change of subject and
grinned at her shyly. "I'm afraid it sounds grander than it

is. Actually, I'm a sort of general dogsbody. But it's a wonderful opportunity to work with Angus and Josh. They're
great."

"Is that what you want to be—a director?"

"I don't know yet." His tone chilled. "I haven't made
up my mind. I'm sort of an apprentice at the moment. Josh
brought me into this, and I was glad to get a chance to—"
He broke off and then went off on a tangent. "Mr. Scrowski wants me to go into the executive side of things, and
I think he may be right. I'm not sure I'd ever be any good
at handling the artistic temperament." A look of acute
misery came into his face.

"Well, I'm sure you'll be very good at anything you
decide on," Penny said, her heart giving a motherly twinge
at his obvious distress. "Dr. White speaks very highly of
your abilities."

"Thank you," he mumbled and got up. "I won't keep
you from your letter, but thanks again."

Penny watched him go, with sympathy. *Poor little devil.
Head over heels in love and can't do a thing about it. What
hell it is to be young.* With a sigh, she turned back to her
maternal duties.

Lunchtime had finally arrived. "There's one thing we
should look into without further ado," Penny said with a
satisfied sigh as she pushed away her empty plate.

Toby, who had, as usual, finished quite some time before
and who had been watching her gourmandizing with a
critical eye, perked up. "What's that?"

"The question of cars," she said. "Thompson and Melody Martin *must* have driven out to the theater—they certainly wouldn't have walked, and I can't see them using
a taxi in those costumes. So either someone took them
or Thompson's murderer removed the car. Therefore, if we
can pin down what cars were available and who had
access to them, we'd be a step closer to our MLS."

"I do wish you wouldn't talk in initials," Toby grumbled. "You know how I feel about bureaucrats. What's
MLS?"

"Most likely suspect, of course!"

"Oh!" He sniffed and produced his little black notebook. "I've already looked into that. Here it is: one car

they brought with them, a special camper for Wolf's equipment, the recording gear and the props; and two others they hired at Izmir, their port of entry, a jeep and a large sedan. Miss de Witt in particular does not approve of jeeps. So there are three vehicles in total."

"And who had the keys?"

"Wolf and Andrew Dale to the camper. Angus McLean and Andrew Dale for the jeep. And Andrew, again, was the keeper of the keys for the sedan, but one pair was always floating around the company somewhere. So that doesn't tell us much."

"Do they all drive?"

"I've nothing definite on that, but presumably they all do—except Josh, of course."

"Joshua White doesn't drive?"

Toby shook his head. "No, it's one of his eccentricities. He hates machines of any kind and never learned. Always had to be chauffeured everywhere on the digs. A crashing bore it was, too."

"So that seems to let him out."

"Possibly." Toby's tone was noncommittal. "He has always been a great walker, though."

"Where were the cars parked?"

"In a parking lot behind the hotel, and to anticipate your next question, I don't know if they were all there yesterday morning. Hamit Bey hasn't got that far yet, or, if he has, he didn't see fit to tell me about it."

"So it breaks down that Josh White is presumably out of it, Andrew Dale had access to all the cars, Wolf and Angus to the camper and jeep respectively, and potentially everyone else to the sedan. It doesn't get us very far, does it?" Penny said gloomily.

"Not yet, but we may have more after I see Hamit again later today. He has promised me a rundown on where everyone says they were during the vital period yesterday."

"So now you're definitely off the hook and promoted to policeman's aide number one!"

"Not entirely," Toby said with a grim smile. "I notice that my digging gloves have disappeared—temporarily, I hope!"

"You mean they've searched your room and taken them?" Penny said with horror.

Toby chuckled. "This isn't England or America, you know. The police here have a lot more latitude."

"Aren't you annoyed?"

"Why should I be? They'll probably test the gloves for powder marks and blood, but they won't find anything and will probably put them back precisely where they found them. I imagine they've searched your things, too—they're still looking for the gun, after all."

"Well, really!" Penny said indignantly. "I think that's the very limit!"

"I wonder what they made of that voodoo doll you always cart around with you." Toby chuckled and then blanched visibly.

Penny glanced over her shoulder and saw Gloria de Witt sweep into the dining room, but the actress's attention was not fixed on them. Instead she was waving a yellow slip of paper in her hand, and she boomed, "Friends, I have just received a cable from Hyman. It is intended for us *all,* so I will read it." Her eyes swept the group to command silence; then she cleared her throat impressively and read, " 'GREETINGS DARLINGS. REGRET UNAVOIDABLY DETAINED BUT HOPE TO BE WITH YOU SOON. KEEP "TELE" ROLLING AND HAVE FUN. HY.' "

"Where was it sent from, Gloria?" Angus McLean's clipped voice broke the dead silence.

Gloria brought the slip of paper closer to her pointed nose. "It's not very clear," she said in a puzzled voice, "but it looks like Palermo, Sicily. Whatever could he be doing there?"

CHAPTER 7

Penny awoke with a heavy head, grimaced with pain as she moved it and lay wondering if she had enough energy to stagger as far as her suitcase for some Bufferin. *You really ought to know better by this time,* she told herself severely, but the previous evening had been so interesting that the after-effects were almost worth it.

She and Toby had been joined at dinner by Josh, who this time had brought along his two companions, Andrew Dale and Angus McLean. After introductions had been made all around—during which she was amused to see Andrew acting as if they had never set eyes on each other before—Joshua and Toby had almost immediately settled into another unending heart-to-heart conversation, and she had been left to entertain Angus and Andrew.

It had been hard going at first; Andrew was very silent, and from time to time she had caught him, the same expression of acute misery on his face, looking over at the table where Carla Vincent, her black eye discreetly shrouded in dark glasses, sat with her husband and Yamura. Angus also had initially been very reserved, and Penny had felt a little inhibited herself by the feeling, common to those first in the presence of a well-known public personality, that in some way she was invading one of his few private moments. As she often did when she was not at ease, she had found herself chattering on about nothing in particular, trying to find some wavelength that would tune Angus in to her.

He was not a typical dour Scot, she thought, but just naturally rather shy and reserved, and nothing about him was obvious, not his age, his feelings or his thoughts. He was essentially an "inward" man, but one she felt would prove extremely interesting once tapped; so she had persevered, until, finally, she struck the right vein when she began to question him on certain philosophical aspects of some of his award-winning films. He had not only responded but had become positively expansive. Flushed by her success, Penny had paraded her knowledge of his less well known achievements to such an extent that he eventually looked at her with a smile in his rather cold gray eyes and said, "I am most flattered that you are so well acquainted with my work, Dr. Spring."

"I've always been very enthusiastic about your films, Mr. McLean. I think I've seen everything you have ever made, and I remember them all vividly," she had said recklessly.

After that the ice was broken, and it was he who had taken the lead in drawing her out. They had ranged over a wide variety of subjects and of places, for he had traveled widely, and the more they talked, the more she had warmed to him. Perhaps a little too much so! she now reflected wryly. After they had finished eating and Andrew had rather abruptly excused himself and left, the other two had gone on talking and drinking; so Angus had also ordered another bottle of the local wine, and they had continued their own tête-à-tête. Almost inevitably their talk had turned to the events of the past two days and, with the wine loosening up her tongue, Penny had said unthinkingly, "Yes, it's a bit of a shock to be practically an eyewitness to a murder."

"Eyewitness!" Angus had said sharply. "You mean you were at the amphitheater when Thompson was murdered?"

"No, I was at the Greek theater when Melody Martin was murdered," she had said, realizing belatedly that she shouldn't have said it.

Toby, who must have been listening in to their conversation with one ear, had turned to glare at her, and Angus had said immediately, "Melody *dead!* Why weren't we informed of this by the police?"

Penny had tried to retrieve her blunder. "Well," she had said weakly, "you see, the body hasn't been found; so they do not entirely credit my story."

"But you saw her murdered? By whom?" Angus had demanded, his eyes an Arctic gray.

"No, I didn't exactly see her murdered. I saw her after," Penny had said feebly. "And I'm afraid I've been rather indiscreet in telling you this; so I'd be most grateful, Angus, if you wouldn't repeat what I've said to anyone until the police are satisfied with their own inquiries." She could tell that he would have liked to ask her more questions, but she had been so shaken by her gaffe that she bade them all a hasty good night and tottered up to bed.

And now, in the early morning hours, she still felt guilty. *Even if Angus does hold his tongue, and I do hope he will,* she thought, *I'm still going to catch hell from Toby. But Angus simply couldn't be involved; he's far too nice.*

Her ruminations were interrupted by a tapping at the door. A glance at her watch confirmed her worst fears. "Oh, no, not him again!" she groaned and tottered out of bed.

"Aren't you ready?" Bilger inquired peevishly when she opened the door.

"Of course not!" Penny moaned. "You don't mean you're going to go through that ridiculous exercise of yesterday *again?*"

"I am until we find the body," Bilger said with some heat. "I thought you understood that."

"Well, *I* don't want to go, and I certainly have no intention of going again without Toby. With just you and me, it is a case of the blind leading the blind—it's hopeless!"

"If I get him to come, will you come?" Bilger asked instantly. "The sooner that body is found, the better it will be for you and everybody."

After last night, you might well be right, she thought. "All right," she assented glumly. "Go get Toby and I'll get ready." She staggered off in search of the Bufferin.

The atmosphere in the jeep was funereal as they made once more for the old city on the hill. Toby slumped in his corner, unshaven and unhappy. Inhibited by Bilger's presence, he hadn't said a word about the events of the night before but contented himself with glaring at Penny and making small hmmphing noises. She slumped in her corner waiting for the weight on top of her head to lift, thinking drearily that she was undoubtedly in for another breakfastless day. Bilger sat hunched over the wheel, glancing impatiently at his watch, obviously most unhappy at having had foisted on him the company of one he believed to be in the camp of the enemy.

When Toby indicated that he wanted to start at the top of the acropolis, Penny and Bilger both protested vigorously that they had already done that and counterproposed that they start on the lower city. Toby let it be known in no uncertain terms that if he was to be dragged from his bed at such an unearthly hour, he fully intended to search systematically or not at all, and he stalked away up the hill. After looking gloomily at one another for a minute, Penny and Bilger trailed obediently after him.

Toby started from the site of the Great Altar and proceeded to quarter the ruins like a bloodhound casting around for a scent. Half an hour passed with no result; still, he stalked on in silence, his eyes fixed firmly on the ground. Suddenly he halted in his tracks, so that Penny, who was following closely behind him, almost ran into him. He was looking fixedly at a circular ring of bare earth in which a few roots of sickly yellow grass raised feeble arms to the sun; then he stepped back and hastily scanned the face of the stone-walled terrace they had been skirting.

"You have found something?" Bilger asked anxiously.

Toby nodded. "I think so. Something large and circular has recently been moved from the grass here, and in this terrace are old burial vaults; so I shouldn't be surprised to find one of them with its entrance sealed—" He let out a pleased exclamation. "There it ·is! Here, come and give me a hand with this!"

"This" was a large, circular slab of stone whose original purpose was probably that of a drain cover, for its top was fashioned into the semblance of a snarling beast, the open mouth of the creature serving as a drain hole. Under the combined efforts of the two men, it rolled easily away from the face of the terrace, revealing the rectangular opening of a small doorway. Toby stooped to enter, then checked himself and took a step backward. He looked grimly at Bilger. "You're the policeman," he said gruffly. "If there's anything in there, you'd better be the first to see it."

Bilger nodded and produced a flashlight from his pocket. Switching it on, he gave them an excited glance and plunged into the darkness. A minute passed while Penny and Toby looked at each other in concerned silence; then Bilger emerged, his olive skin now a greenish white. In his hand he was clutching a large white handbag. "She's in there," he said in a choked voice, "and even though we know she has been moved, she had better not be moved again until our technical men have had a look."

"It's Melody Martin?" Penny said, a quiver in her voice.

"Well, it's the girl you described, down to the last detail," Bilger muttered, "but I don't think I'll ask you to identify her; decomposition has started, and it is not a very pleasant sight." He swallowed hard, then gathered himself together and held up the handbag. "However, this was beside her, and I see no harm in a preliminary examination of its contents while we are on the spot."

He reached in his pocket and brought out a large white handkerchief, which he spread on the ground. Kneeling down, he carefully tipped the contents of the bag onto it and sat back on his heels looking thoughtfully at the small pile of objects, among them the familiar green of an American passport. Behind her, Penny heard Toby draw in his breath sharply, and she glanced at him in time to see his expression change from one of concern to enigmatic blankness.

Bilger took two small objects from the pile, examined them closely and then held them out to Toby, a curious look on his face. "Do you know what these are?"

Toby was silent for a moment, examining the little figurines as they glinted in the sun. "I think so," he said carefully. "Do you?"

"I have seen similar ones, but not in gold. These *are* gold, aren't they?"

Toby took the objects from him and examined them more closely. "Possibly—or it might be electrum. One couldn't tell without analysis."

Penny leaned forward and peered at them.

"Would you be able to put a date on them?" Bilger asked.

"Not precisely, but the style is almost certainly early Hittite."

"And the subjects?"

"The man standing on the bull is Teshub; the woman

with the child in her arms is the Hittite version of the mother goddess. Together they make the 'holy family' of the Hittites."

"This isn't Hittite country."

"I know, so presumably Miss Martin must have obtained them somewhere else in Turkey."

Bilger was leafing rapidly through the passport. "She entered Turkey at Istanbul by plane and proceeded to Izmir with only a transit stop at Yesilkoy airport."

"Maybe she bought them from a dealer as souvenirs."

"When?" Bilger snapped. "She arrived at Izmir late in the evening, stayed with the company at the hotel and came on to Bergama the next morning—the day she was killed. Anyway, you probably know as well as I do, Dr. Glendower, that the sale of precious antiquities such as these appear to be is strictly against Turkish law. The only way she could have bought these would be illegally —*if* she bought them," he added half to himself. "And why should she be carrying them around just loose like that?"

"Why couldn't she just have found them?" Penny queried.

The two men looked at her as if they had forgotten she was there. Toby said in a pained voice, "Well, in the first place there is the time factor, as pointed out, and in the second place this whole area, Izmir and Bergama included, always lay outside the limits of the Hittite empire; so it just isn't very likely she found them lying around here."

His gaze held a warning in it, so Penny said hastily, indicating the passport, "What was her real name? I'd like to know."

Bilger consulted it again. "Surprisingly enough, Melody Martin. Born in Brooklyn, New York, twenty-five years old, one hundred twenty pounds, five feet five and one half inches tall, blond hair, brown eyes, no distinguishing marks."

"*Brown* eyes! So much for my perfect Nordic type," Penny said ruefully.

"Hello! Here's an envelope addressed to her, care of the Izmir hotel they stayed at," Bilger said, "and it's empty. Anyone recognize the writing?" They shook their heads. "Everything else seems to be pretty ordinary: handkerchief, cosmetics, bottle of prescription pills, change purse, traveler's checks, American cigarettes, cigarette lighter." He held up the little gold object. "Hmmm, inscribed 'BR TO MM—WITH LOVE.' Something else to look into." He sighed and tipped the objects back into the bag, then scrambled to his feet. "We'd better get going back to town, and I think, just to be on the safe side, we'd better cover the opening again. I'll drop you back at the hotel, but we'll probably need you down at the station later, Dr. Spring, to make a full statement about Tuesday's events now that the body has been found. I need hardly tell you to say nothing about all this to the people at the hotel." Penny had the grace to blush.

Her statement was eventually taken by a far more affable Hamit Bey than she had seen up to that point, and he unbent so far as to tell her that the autopsy on the dead actress was taking place at that very moment and to entrust her with a sheaf of papers for Toby. "Information requested," he said briefly.

"It's the rundown on the alibis for Tuesday morning," Toby said enthusiastically when she offered him this placebo. "At last, something to get our teeth into! Let's go somewhere quiet and go over them now. Your room or mine?" They decided on hers.

Since the papers were in Turkish, Toby settled down to translate, Penny to transcribe. After a steady two hours of work and a severe case of writer's cramp on her part, they sat back to survey their efforts.

Toby lit up his inevitable pipe and settled himself more comfortably in his chair. "So—they came as a group from Rome to Istanbul and from there to Izmir. The group stayed in two different hotels in Izmir, reason unknown, and there seems to be a certain amount of confusion as to who went with whom on the trip over here." He wrinkled his brow. "Let's see, Angus left earlier than the rest, bringing Andrew Dale, Josh, and the art director, Yamura, with him in the jeep. The camper, which also took most of the baggage, left next, and because it was so full, Wolf Vincent only brought his wife and Gale Thompson. The rest were supposed to come in the sedan driven by Brett Russell, but—" He whistled softly to himself. "Gloria de Witt states there was no sign of Thompson or Melody when it came time to go, and Brett Russell told her that Thompson had said to go on and they'd be along later. Now, according to Russell, the last time he saw Thompson, the latter was dressed in ordinary street clothes. Thompson had collared Russell in the hotel lobby to say that Melody was not ready, because she had risen late, and since he had some business to do in Izmir, he'd hire a car and he and Melody would come along later.

"Izmir's just under sixty miles from Bergama—say, about an hour's drive. So McLean left at seven and got here about eight-fifteen A.M., Vincent left at seven-forty-five and arrived at eight-forty-five, and Russell left about eight-fifteen and got here at nine-thirty."

"So Thompson just *couldn't* have been far behind him," Penny interjected. "Not if he were to get changed, up to the theater, commit a murder and dump the body by ten-thirty. And, anyway, where's the hired car?"

"Yes, that is strange," Toby mused. "Unless he hired a car with a driver, which seems a bit senseless. And whatever his business was, it couldn't have taken much time, as you say."

"What about the alibis for the time of Thompson's murder?" Penny asked.

"Well, let's take them in order." Toby shuffled the papers into a neat pile and started to make notes in his black notebook. "Um, Brett Russell says he went straight to his room on arrival and unpacked his suitcases; then he lay down and read a book until lunchtime at one. No confirmation of this other than the boy at the hotel who carried his bags up at nine-thirty A.M.

"Did he still have the keys to the sedan?"

"Apparently so—at least it doesn't say."

"Gloria de Witt says she went to her room and 'meditated' until lunchtime. Again unconfirmed, other than her arrival."

"Angus McLean and Josh checked in, confirmed the reservations for everybody and then took the jeep out for a ride around, looking for a suitable place for one of the new episodes in the script. Returned at one-thirty P.M. for lunch."

"So that lets them out, I suppose, since they alibi one another," Penny said doubtfully.

"Unless they happen to be in collusion," Toby said quietly. "I can tell you, those figurines gave me a nasty jolt this morning. It really brings the smuggling motive right into the forefront again."

"I still can't see how it could possibly fit in."

"All right—just supposing, mind you—but what if Josh was up to something along this line, as he has been before, and the girl somehow stumbled across it? If she was a blackmailer, as has been hinted, maybe she was trying to blackmail Josh."

"But that means he *and* Angus would have to be involved, as well as Thompson, and I just can't believe that!"

"Agreed, it doesn't seem very *likely*," Toby sighed, "but still it can't be completely ruled out."

"And what about Andrew Dale?"

"He took care of one or two minor business details, helped Vincent unload the baggage from the camper and then, at nine-thirty, 'went for a walk' and did not get back until lunchtime."

"Where did he go?"

"Not downtown, evidently, but just out into the country. The statement is very vague. Wolf Vincent, after unloading the camper, had a drink with his wife and Gale Thompson, then said he had to check over some of the props and cameras and went back to the camper. According to him, this took him until lunchtime, but there's an interesting item here from one of the hotel cooks that says he heard the camper—which makes a rather distinctive noise—being driven up to the back of the hotel just before one o'clock. Unfortunately, he did not see it, nor can he say when it left.

"Carla Vincent says she went downtown for some shopping, after the drinks with her husband, and then came back and wrote some letters in the hotel lounge until lunchtime."

"Then, she must have a lousy sense of smell," Penny said stoutly. "That room hadn't been aired for I don't know how long when I used it the next day, and I had a hell of a time getting any of the windows open."

"Hmm." Toby was again noncommittal. "Anyway, Gale

Thompson does confirm the first part of her story in that she says they walked together downtown and then separated. She says she picked up a couple of items from the local chemist's and came back to her room, where she still was when the police came to inform her of her husband's death. Hamit Bey has a little note to the effect that the news did not seem to come as a shock to her."

"And Yamura?"

"After he arrived with McLean, no one saw him, and he claims he walked down to the river and did some sketching. This again has no sort of confirmation."

"So what it boils down to," Penny said, "is that *no one* —with the possible exception of Angus and Joshua—has any kind of solid alibi for the vital period."

"Devilish but true," Toby agreed gloomily. "But, then, few people, however innocent, can usually provide alibis at a moment's notice, and they can't all be guilty. There are a couple of interesting pointers, though: at least two of these people seemingly lied."

"You mean Wolf Vincent about the camper?"

"Yes, that is one instance. If the hotel cook is correct, then someone was driving it; so it was either Wolf himself, or he wasn't working in it as long as he claims and someone else took it in his absence. Either way, he lied."

"And the other?"

"Gloria de Witt."

"Gloria?"

"Yes. Nowhere does she mention the fact that during the time she was supposed to be meditating, she was up and about the hotel, since she collared *me* about ten o'clock."

"Maybe that was just an oversight," Penny muttered. "Also, it puts her in the clear for Melody Martin's murder. You're her alibi, and it seems a bit absurd to suppose she went straight from chasing you to shooting Thompson."

Toby chuckled grimly. "Yes, it does seem a rather sudden change of emphasis—unless she is completely mad, of course. She could have followed me and then shot him in an excess of racial rage. Still, enough of useless speculation. Time we got back to work again."

"Oh? I thought we'd done our bit for the day."

"If·it is not too late already, I'd like to sound out some

of these people before the news of Melody Martin's murder comes out. I feel our next joint target should be the Vincents. I'd very much like to know why Wolf lied in his original statement to the police, and you could be well employed getting to know Mrs. Vincent. From what little I've seen of her, she strikes me as a young woman with a lot on her mind, and well worth a visit, if you follow me."

"I follow you," Penny said absently. She was thinking of the little tableau she had witnessed the day before. What if that had not been the first but the second act of a drama enacted before on the same spot? And in the intermission somebody had given Carla Vincent that black eye!

Their detecting plans however were destined to come to naught, for they descended from Penny's room to find that the entire company had been summoned to the police station. The assistant manager was agog with the news. "They say," he confided, "that there has been a big new development."

Toby and Penny looked innocently interested. "Oh, and what's that?"

"Well, I don't know for sure, but it is something to do with blood."

"Blood!" they echoed in chorus.

"Yes!" He leaned toward them confidentially. "They were all asked to go down to the police station and make complete statements, and all the men are to have their blood tested. I've no idea why."

CHAPTER 8

"Oh, that poor, poor girl!" Gloria de Witt's voice sank into the tenor range as she made this pronouncement, one that she had repeated every five minutes since her return. The women had returned and were now huddled in a protective group in the dining room, which had become the group's focal point simply because there was no other place for them to gather. The hotel, standing as it did on the outskirts of Bergama, was to all intents and purposes a "country" hotel—quite unlike the luxurious Western-style hotels of Istanbul. It was clean; bare and Spartan in its appointments, the tiny lounge having obviously been added as an afterthought by a management hopeful for, but not really anticipating, an influx of non-Turkish visitors. The middle-class Turks who normally frequented it expected a clean bed to sleep in and a clean dining room in which to both eat and socialize, and this is precisely what they got. With the rapid adaptability of the human species, the foreigners had accepted the conditions which, in their own countries, would have sent them screaming for the manager or to another hotel in no time at all. So now the women were seated on the black hardwood chairs around a plastic-topped square table, denuded of its usual white mealtime covering. Penny had firmly added herself to the group as mass-sympathizer and finder-of-the-body.

For one thing, she did not much fancy being alone. The morning's activities had upset her more than she cared to admit, and she also hoped to glean some interesting facts from this all-female tête-à-tête.

She had given them a terse account of the grisly find on the acropolis and then had become determinedly silent in the hopes of drawing them out. Gloria had been very much "onstage" since the return, addressing the bulk of her remarks to Penny, as the other two sat glumly by.

Both of them—Carla, still shrouded in her dark glasses, and Gale, her black eyes smoldering—had so far been uncommunicative. They replied when directly addressed, but in monosyllables, and Penny sensed, in addition to the dislike they evidently felt for the old actress, an undercurrent of hostility to each other.

She had been encouraging Gloria in her performance, hoping that in all that flood of verbiage some interesting fact might emerge, but, in truth, she was listening with only half an ear. The rest of her thoughts dwelt upon what might be happening at the police station, where the men were still being interrogated.

"She was so young, so vital, so interested in *life,* so interested in people. We all felt it, men and women alike—that she was interested in one for oneself alone; that one's joy were her joys, one's sorrows her sorrows. She was someone one could open one's very heart to—"

"Yeah—she was a real snoop," Gale's Australian twang cut in.

Gloria ignored her. "And such acting potential! This banal movie came alive every time she was on camera. And she was a cameraman's dream! Not a bad camera angle from top to toe. No wonder Wolf was so crazy about her." She paused dramatically, as if caught in an indiscretion, and then said, "I hope you don't mind my saying that, Carla. I didn't mean . . ."

"Why should I mind?" The girl's voice was shrill with stress. "She was beautiful—no one can deny that—but 'crazy' is hardly the word to use for Wolf. He's a professional through and through and appreciated her as that, nothing more."

"Oh, quite!" Gloria purred. "I didn't mean to upset you further. I mean, you were so upset when she replaced you."

"Look, you know as well as I do, Gloria, that I didn't care all that much about the lead—it was Hyman and Wolf who cooked that up. It was just the way I got pushed out that made us both mad. That plus all the extra work the damn changes entailed."

Gloria glanced significantly at Penny and went on hurriedly, "Well, I agree with you, some of the changes were *totally* unnecessary"—she threw a venomous glance at Gale, who glared back—"and did *nothing* for the picture.

But now"—she stopped and pressed a hand to her breast—
"it is of no consequence. It is all over. Finished. Without
her we *cannot* go on." Her head drooped in sorrow. It was
evidently an exit line.

Penny came to with a start and said, "Er—have you
managed to contact Mr. Scrowski yet?"

Gloria's already furrowed brow furrowed still more.
"No," she said in a normal, worried voice, "and I just
can't understand it. I tried to contact him in Palermo and
could find no trace of him. He's gone—*if* he was ever
there at all," she added ominously.

"If? You mean you don't think that cable was from
him?"

"I don't know," Gloria said unhappily. "There were
three redundant words in that cable, and that just isn't
like Hy, not like him at all." She sighed heavily. "Well, if
we can't find him, I suppose I'll have to take it upon myself
to get the company back to Marseilles as soon as possible.
There is no use sitting around here running up useless ex-
penses."

"You can forget that penny-pinching pipe dream in a
hurry," Gale's voice broke in. "You don't think they're
going to let us go before they find which one of us is the
murderer, do you?"

The hand flew to the heart again. "Oh, no! One of *our*
little company the murderer!" Gloria exclaimed in horror.

"Oh, come off it, Gloria!" Now it was Carla's turn.
"Can't you face up to the fact that it almost has to be one
of us? Someone among us has taken two lives, and until
that someone is found . . ." Her voice quavered and broke,
but both girls continued to stare, flint-eyed, at the old
actress.

"Oh, no—this is *too* much!" Gloria's voice swelled. "I
just cannot accept that. The police will find the culprit—
undoubtedly some local sneak thief! In these barbaric
countries such things are a common occurrence. No, I will
not for one moment believe one of *us* is responsible."

You didn't sing that tune the other night, Penny thought.
*And, what's more, now you are overacting, and overacting
badly. I wonder why?*

The acrimonious hassle that was developing among the
three women was abruptly cut short by the noisy eruption

of the men into the dining room. Angus McLean strode over to their table, his sandy hair as ruffled as his usual calm. "Gloria, I've got to talk to you. We've simply *got* to find Scrowski, and we've also got to get ourselves a lawyer." He bore her away.

Penny was covertly watching the two girls and was interested to see that Carla's worried gaze immediately flew to the quietly tense Andrew, and Gale's to the lithe figure of Carla's husband, who came striding over to them. "Have either of you seen Telemachus's dagger?" he demanded. "It was in the inventory when we left Marseilles, and now the police have been asking for it and I can't seem to find it."

The eagle's glare swept over them searchingly, but both girls shook their heads, and Gale volunteered, "Last time I saw it, it was with all the rest of the things, but that was in Marseilles."

"Well, come with me now, will you, and we'll check again."

Carla got up to join them, and her husband barked at her, "No, we don't need you. I'll see you later." She flinched at his tone and turned away, her hands tightening into fists.

Penny saw Toby beckoning to her from the doorway and hastily excused herself. She found Josh with him. "What's been happening?" she demanded. "What's all the excitement about?"

"Some rather startling developments," Toby said drily. "They've kept Brett Russell down at the station, and if he doesn't come up with some answers pretty fast, I think they are going to arrest him."

"Brett Russell! For the murders? But why?"

They hustled her into the small lounge and closed the door behind them. "Mainly because Brett Russell has AB-positive blood and no one else here has," Toby said grimly.

"But what has that got to do with it?"

"The autopsy revealed, among other things, that Melody Martin was three month's pregnant, and a blood sampling of the fetus showed it was also AB-positive. She was an O-positive. That, plus the gold lighter Bilger found in her bag, has led the police to cast Brett Russell as suspect number one."

"I can scarcely credit it," Penny said slowly.

"Nor I," Josh White barked. "A lot of bloody nonsense, if you ask me. Brett Russell is no killer. After all, he's not the only AB-positive man in the world. And even if he did knock the girl up, why murder her? One wife or scandal more or less wouldn't have done *him* any harm."

"There is the factor that he has been extremely hard-pressed for money for some time," Toby said slowly. "And, also—this is according to Angus McLean—he's been romancing a very wealthy divorcée in the south of France. A scandal of any kind may have put an end to that."

"Yes, but why should he kill Thompson?" Penny said. "That doesn't make any sense at all."

"Not unless your theory was right all along—that Thompson saw the first murder done and so had to be silenced," Toby said. "You were right about the wound, too. It was not inflicted by Thompson's sword but by a thin-bladed dagger. There were two of those in the props here—one that Brett Russell wore and Thompson's—and neither can be found. The police are now mounting a more intensive search for both them and the gun. Also, Brett Russell's lack of a positive alibi for Tuesday morning doesn't augur very well for him. He had access to the sedan, you remember, though now he denies having the keys. Says he gave them back to young Andrew as soon as he got in."

"And what does Andrew say?"

"That he can't remember. There was so much hurly-burly going on when they first arrived at the hotel, particularly after the luggage arrived, that he says he may have got them back and given them out again without noticing. He can only produce the one set of keys."

Penny sighed. "I still find it rather hard to accept. I mean, *why* should Brett have taken both Thompson and Melody up to the Greek theater and murdered her then? Also, what happened to the car they came from Izmir in? And what about the evidence of the camper? And what about 'mammoth'? If Russell were Thompson's killer, why didn't he just say 'Brett' or 'Russell'?"

"Yes, there are quite a few loose ends the police will have to tie up before they've got any sort of case," Toby agreed. "And I must say, neither he nor his motive seems highly likely to me. Oh, there was one other thing that came out at the autopsy which might interest you: that blue contact lens—it was Melody's. She was still wearing the other one. In fact, most of the people here believed her to be blue-eyed."

"You know, I'm getting the strangest feelings about her," Penny said. "It's hard to put into words exactly, but —well, about the lens, it was almost as if she were trying to be the ideal Nordic type for someone. And being pregnant. I mean, *no one* nowadays needs to get pregnant unless she wants to, or to continue the pregnancy if it is not what she wants, and it certainly isn't a viable instrument for a shotgun marriage anymore. And on top of that, Gloria told me that she was very sympathetic and a good listener."

"I really don't see what you're getting at," Toby said in a puzzled tone.

"I'm not exactly sure myself," Penny confessed, "but it's as if she were trying rather desperately to please or to belong to someone or something—almost frantically so. By the way, did they find out what was in those prescription pills?"

"Uppers, apparently." Toby cleared his throat emphatically, which was a sure sign he did not want to go on with this particular subject. "A lot of actresses take them, I believe, to stimulate their performance."

Penny took the hint and changed the subject. "So now what's the position? What's going to happen?"

"We're still stuck here," Josh rasped. "Nothing has changed. If they charge Brett, they may let us go, but I think they'll find they haven't got enough to charge him with; so they'll still keep us hanging. God, what a mess! I don't know about you two, but I could use a drink, a double at that." His eyebrows were fiercely inquiring.

"Not just now, Josh, thanks," Toby said absently. "Penny and I are going for a walk."

"We are?" Penny said after the door had closed behind the old archaeologist.

"Not really, but I wanted to get rid of him. He's been sticking to me closer than glue," Toby said petulantly. "I couldn't even get a word with Bilger about the figurines, which have been sent off to the Izmir museum for examination."

"You know, that's another thing that doesn't add up or make any sense," Penny remarked. "If there's anything in your theory that antiquity smuggling is mixed up in all this somehow and was the motive for the murder, why didn't the murderer remove the figurines from the bag?"

Toby sighed. "At this stage we just don't know, but I can think of at least two explanations. For instance, Thompson was the murderer of Melody Martin but realized the significance of the figurines he found in her bag, hid them with her and started a bit of blackmail on his account and so got himself killed. *Or* whoever did the murder never thought she would be so foolish as to carry the figurines around with her like that and just overlooked them in his haste to get the body out of sight."

"That doesn't hold water," Penny said quickly. "You're forgetting the empty envelope. No woman carts around an empty envelope in her bag unless it's for the return address, and that *had* no return address. Whoever put her in that tomb must have looked in her bag, and if he took the letter that envelope contained, he'd have seen the figurines."

"You've got a point there," Toby said gloomily. "So there's nothing for it but to get back to work. I think I'll go and lurk around Wolf Vincent for a bit. I noticed he got very rattled when the police started to question him about the props for the picture—the daggers, and so on. Since they had already made it pretty clear that they suspected Brett, I found that rather odd. What are you going to do?"

"I think I'll have another heart-to-heart with Gale Thompson," Penny said. "There is something funny going on between her and the Vincents, and I'm not sure what."

She found her quarry looking tensely out of the window of her room, which Penny had entered in response to a terse "Come in." Gale merely glanced over her shoulder to see who had answered her summons, before taking up her contemplative stance once more. In this case a direct approach would probably be the best, Penny decided. "I'd like to talk to you, Mrs. Thompson. To lay it right on the line, I don't think Mr. Russell was responsible for your husband's death, and I don't think you believe that, either. I know this is an extremely difficult time for you, but if any of us are ever going to get away from here, the truth *has* to be discovered; and, to do that, I am simply going to have to know more about your husband."

"To get out of here." The black girl turned a woebegone face to her. "Yes, that's what I want; that's all that I want, Dr. Spring." Her knuckles showed almost white as she clenched her fists. "I guess you're about the only one around here who can understand what I'm feeling just now, Dr. Spring. I'm a full-blooded lubra and, believe me, the urge for a walkabout now is driving me crazy! Let's get out of here and go for a walk. I'm so mixed up that I can't even think with these walls closing me in." She grinned suddenly. "Don't worry, I'm not going to take off all my clothes in the public street. They're at least weaned *that* urge out of me."

They walked out of the hotel in a silence, which Gale finally broke. She began almost dreamily. "You know, my grandfather was the one who realized none of us would have any future if we didn't give up the old way of life. He managed to set himself up in a little sheep station and kept at it until, by the time he died, it was a big sheep station. But my grandmother told me there were times— particularly when he had a lot on his mind—that this look would come into his eyes, and she would hear him get up in the night and put on his old breechclout and all the insignia of the old life and start walking around the out- side of the house. She'd get up and see him walking there in the moonlight, around and around and around, until he was ready to drop with exhaustion; but he never allowed himself to leave the station, not once. I think he knew that if he did allow himself to return to the old ways just one time, he'd never be able to come back." She paused. "I used to think that was such a funny story when I was young, but now I know exactly how he felt."

"You were very fond of your husband, weren't you?" Penny said softly.

"I loved the man he *was;* I'm not so sure about the man he had become—but, yes, I was."

"What was he like?"

"I don't really know," Gale said surprisingly. "Our

backgrounds were too different for me to know what he really felt or thought about anything. But he was bright—he wasn't one of those superjocks who are all show on the outside and nothing between the ears. I guess what he really lacked was complete confidence in himself. He had to be up front, right where he'd be noticed. He needed to make it big, not just because he was black or a militant—he wasn't—or anything like that, but just for himself. The pressures of pro football got to be too much for him, I suppose, and, like so many others, he started on pep pills so he'd feel great for the games. He just wasn't very lucky, that's all. When the dope scandal came out, the others who had been on the stuff a lot longer got away with it, but he got canned. He changed after that, sort of closed up inside himself—got meaner, too. Wouldn't talk much anymore and got mixed up with a crowd I never even got to see. He'd be away from home sometimes a week at a time, and when he came back, no explanation, no nothing. I thought it was another woman at first, but I don't think it ever was. I even offered to let him out, but he didn't want that. In fact, he seemed to cling to me in an odd sort of way. Then, about six months ago, I found out that uppers hadn't been enough for him and that he really had a monkey on his back. He'd never talk about it, but I knew by the rate we were going through our savings how bad it was. Although I've bitched enough about this lousy picture, it was a lifesaver in a way. We'd have hit bottom without it. It did something for him, too. He started talking big again, said we'd soon be all set financially, and then he'd go for a cure and kick the habit—even talked about getting into shape again and going back into football. . . ." She trailed into silence.

"And you never met any of these—er—contacts that he had for the drugs?" Penny queried.

"No, not once. But I do know when he got picked up with the stuff in his car that time in L.A., someone saw that he got a good lawyer fast. He just wouldn't tell me a thing about it."

"And how did he get involved in this present business?"

"I don't rightly know that, either. He'd made a big thing at the start as to how he was through with sports and was going to be a big star like Poitier or Rountree, but the truth of it was that he only had one or two bit parts—nothing that amounted to anything. When the big companies could have some of the big black names just for the asking, they weren't too interested in a has-been with a problem like his. As to who first contacted him from this outfit, I think it was McLean, but that was understandable enough, because they wanted a giant. Did you know he actually played in elevator shoes for this thing? Those shoes and the helmet made him seven-foot-six. And, as I've said, he jumped at it because it was a lifesaver. God, that's funny when you think about it!"

"But I understand he didn't get on very well with Mc-Lean," Penny murmured.

"Yes, that's true enough. He got across nearly everyone. Partly it was because he didn't think the role was much. After he got into it, he tried to talk it up and didn't get anywhere. That raddled old bitch didn't help, either, with all her dirty cracks about 'inferior races.' That really got his goat, and he started to throw his weight around just to show her. The habit sort of made him unpredictable, too. One moment he'd be all chummy with someone like Melody and Andrew, and the next thing you knew, he'd be yelling at them and going on like a madman. He started getting all sorts of crazy ideas, even about Wolf and me."

"And was there anything to give him cause?" Penny inquired mildly.

The girl gave her an unfathomable glance. "Nothing that anyone would understand," she said briefly. "Wolf's been a good friend to me; that's all there is to it, whatever they may think." Suddenly she halted and turned abruptly back toward the hotel. "I don't suppose any of this has been any help to you, Dr. Spring, but it's been a help to me just talking about it a bit. I've got to sort things out—they're all mixed up in my mind—and I've got to get away from here to do it. I've just *got* to have a walkabout." There was a note of desperation in her voice. "I can't talk anymore now, but there's one more thing I want you to know—I never wanted him dead. Remember that!" And she walked swiftly away, leaving Penny standing in the road gazing worriedly after her.

Toby was waiting rather disconsolately for Penny when

she got back to the hotel. He had got nowhere with Wolf Vincent, who had brushed him off decisively and then left for parts unknown. Feeling somewhat deflated herself, Penny filled Toby in on her conversation with Gale Thompson; it did nothing to improve his spirits. "So we still know nothing about Thompson and his drug connections," he reflected.

"Not much more, no, except that, like Melody, our second victim does seem to have had a nicer side to him," Penny said. "I'm beginning to like our murderer less and less in consequence, and I really wish I could think of some way to help that poor girl. She's going through a little private hell at the moment."

Toby was suddenly restless. "I could use a break from all this. Let's go for a walk and do some sight-seeing. After all, damn it, it's what we came here for, and we haven't seen a single thing as yet."

They went for their walk, ending up in the basilica. Once safely back in the past, Toby soon regained his usual good humor. As he droned on and walked on, however, Penny became more and more conscious of her aching feet, so that it was with considerable relief that a sudden cloudburst, accompanied by sight-and-sound effects supplied by Zeus in a fine frenzy, caused them to seek shelter under a colonnade of the basilica. As Toby's scholastic monologue droned on, Penny sat on a pillar and rubbed her tired feet, conjuring up in her mind the touching little tableau between Andrew and Carla Vincent that she had unwittingly interrupted. *He certainly was in a temper,* she reflected. *He looked as if he could cheerfully* murder someone. She stopped, appalled at her own thought.

The lightning flashed and the thunder crashed and the rain continued to pour down in sheets. Even under the protection of the colonnade, they were beginning to feel distinctly damp and chilly, and Penny saw with misgivings the hands of her watch creeping around to dinnertime. She had missed her breakfast, as she had feared, and the events of the morning had left her without her usual enthusiasm for lunch; so now she was ravenous again. "If this keeps up, we'll be late for dinner," she said, breaking into Toby's continuing soliloquy. "Do you think we should make a run for it?"

"We'll be drenched through before we go ten steps," Toby replied. He was slightly huffy at having been recalled from the fourth century B.C. for such an inconsequential item as food.

"I certainly don't intend to miss dinner," Penny said firmly. "I've starved quite enough in Bergama already."

"I have never understood how anyone as small as you can eat so much and so constantly," Toby said severely. "Why, I remember one time on a dig in the Zagros Mountains when supplies ran out and *I* went without food for three days and didn't miss it a bit."

"Then, there must have been plenty of drink left," Penny snapped. "I've gone without food, too! In fact, *you've* never lived on snake meat for a whole week, which is what I had to do once. But when it's not necessary to starve, I don't. What's more, I hate to miss anything I've paid for."

Toby sniffed. "Anyway, there's still plenty of time. No sense in getting wet needlessly."

A strained silence ensued, but when the rain continued its unabated drumming and there was no sign of a break in the lowering thunderclouds overhead, he was urged into action by his hungry companion, and they arrived back at the hotel breathless and dripping.

Trails of water in the hotel foyer and up the stairs indicated that they were not the only victims of Zeus's sudden wrath, and they departed separately in search of hot baths and dry clothes.

The atmosphere in the dining room was dismal. People had been trickling in slowly, looking chilly and oppressed by the damp, greenish gloom that hung over everything; conversation was minimal and subdued. Most tables were vacant, Penny noted; so either their usual inhabitants had already eaten and gone or were even more tardy than they. There was no sign of Gloria or of the Vincents or of Yamura and Gale Thompson. Brett Russell, apparently, was still being held by the police; no one had any direct news of him.

Suddenly, so suddenly that they all jumped convulsively, the door flew open, and the figure of Carla Vincent appeared in it, water cascading from her. Her classical features, the black eye now unashamedly bared, were stricken with anguish, and she rushed over to their table, her breath coming in great sobbing gasps.

Andrew sprang up, overturning his chair in the process, but it was not to him she turned. "Angus," she cried, "I'm worried out of my mind. It's Wolf and Gale—they've gone! I've searched everywhere for them, and there's not a sign of them. What's more, the camper is missing. I think we should call the police."

CHAPTER 9

The storm had come and gone, and so had the police; the sun had returned with the daylight, but the missing couple had not. They had disappeared as if by magic.

Nerves were fraying fast, and Toby and Bilger had got into a snarling match. "I thought the police were keeping her under surveillance, as I suggested," Toby challenged.

"We did, up until the time we detained Brett Russell," Bilger snapped back. "Then it was no longer considered necessary, since we were satisfied we had our murderer."

"And now?"

"The situation about Russell is basically unchanged. We have no notion why these two have gone off; it may be a purely personal matter and totally unconnected with what has gone before. Naturally, since they were both warned not to leave Bergama until further notice, they will have to be found and brought back; but so far they are guilty of nothing more serious than a misdemeanor. We have alerted the Izmir police to keep a watch out for them. They may just have gone there on an overnight binge."

"Highly unlikely under the circumstances." Toby sniffed. "I consider a very serious blunder has been made by you, and if anything has happened to that girl, I shall certainly hold you to blame for it. As I indicated to Hamit Bey yesterday, your case against Brett Russell is as full of holes as a Swiss cheese; so to have kept up the surveillance would have been the most elementary precaution."

"And may I remind you, *Bay* Glendower, that you are not the police, who have a far greater scope for information than you can possibly have, and that we know what we are doing."

"I certainly hope so," Toby snapped, and on the wrangle went.

Penny kept very quiet, not wanting to exacerbate a

situation already strained enough. Inwardly she was very worried, and to the worry was added the pricking of a tender conscience: she had omitted to pass on to Toby Gale's conversation—now highly significant—about taking a walkabout. She tried to tell herself it probably was the explanation for their sudden disappearance, that Gale had somehow persuaded Wolf to take her away while she straightened herself out, but this facile explanation did not really submerge a deeper foreboding that things were not to be that simply dismissed. She felt herself sinking hopelessly into a quagmire of conflicting thoughts and theories, and a sense of helplessness seized her. Was she worried *for* Gale or *about* her? And what of Wolf Vincent?

One thing had struck her forcibly when Carla made her dramatic announcement the evening before: no one in that dining room had been at all surprised by it. And she had watched with interest and empathy their various reactions; she had felt the quiet, white-hot anger in Andrew as he tried to comfort the distraught Carla, and a strange sense of desperation in Angus. Josh's reaction had puzzled her the most: he seemed inwardly gleeful at the turn of events. And Gloria de Witt, when she swept upon the scene, had been so triumphantly "I told you so" that she had got into an acrimonious exchange with Andrew and Angus. It was during this minor battle that she had hurled a startling accusation at Angus McLean. "I'm tired of being played for a sucker," she had shrilled. "I don't know what you're up to, Angus, but I'm damned sure you know where Hy is, and I want to know, d'you here? I'm damned if I'm going to be kept in the dark any longer. What have you done with him?" And though Angus had turned Gloria's barb scoffingly aside, Penny felt that the accusation had hit a vulnerable spot, for shortly thereafter he detached himself from the fray and disappeared.

The current argument between Toby and Bilger was brought to a sudden end by the arrival of a sullen-looking constable who took Bilger aside and muttered in his ear, whereupon Bilger gave an excited exclamation and went rushing out. Toby let out a disgusted snort and turned to Penny. "Too much to expect, of course, that he'd pass on the cause of the excitement. It looks as if I'd better pay my daily call on Hamit Bey to find out what's going on. Coming?"

Penny shook her head. "No, I think you do better on your own. I'm so confused at the moment that I've got a splitting headache. I think I'll go and write some letters. I always find that soothing." They went their separate ways.

Toby found Hamit Bey in a state of great good humor, so much so that he was more interested in giving than receiving information, a fact that relieved Toby immensely, since he had very little to offer. "The case is developing very well." Hamit Bey beamed. "Two excellent bits of news. The Izmir police have located the taxi that brought Thompson and Miss Martin from Izmir to Bergama. The taximan's statement is most interesting." He picked up a piece of paper as Toby made encouraging noises behind his smoke screen. "He says that he was hired by a very pretty young woman—by his description, obviously Miss Martin—who engaged him to drive herself and a very large black man to Bergama. She had some difficulty getting the black man into the car because he, according to the driver, was acting very strangely, laughing a lot and very boisterous and excited."

"Sounds as if he'd just had his shot," Toby commented mildly.

"Evidently." Hamit nodded agreement. "He goes on to say that the black man calmed down a bit during the trip but was doing a lot of talking in a loud voice, and though the driver understands only a few words of English and couldn't follow what was said, he got the impression that the girl was egging the man on to talk, playing up to him sexually, and so on, so much so that the black was getting really grabby about her at the end of the drive."

"What time does he say he got here?" Toby interjected.

"Yes—well, here's where it really gets interesting," Hamit said with enthusiasm. "He says he thinks they arrived just after nine-forty-five, though he didn't pay too much attention to the actual time, and instead of delivering them to the front of the hotel as he had intended, they indicated at the last minute that they wanted to go round to the back. Both of them were laughing very hard, he says. There they paid him his money without so much as a

quibble, which surprised him because he'd asked a ridiculous amount for the trip in the first place and then had
demanded a tip on top of it, and they had paid it all. The
Negro was flashing quite a wad of money. The taximan
found it so hard to believe that anyone could be so stupid
that he watched where they went—still both laughing like
anything—and he says they went into a big van parked
at the back of the hotel. He thought that the girl was
probably a prostitute and the man was going to 'make her'
in the van. Anyway, when they didn't come out again, he
just left; so he didn't see anything else."

"Hmm. Very interesting, indeed. That certainly seems to
let Mr. Russell off, doesn't it?" Toby mused.

Hamit Bey looked at him, his grin fading. "Oh? How
so? I don't see that it makes much difference. Russell has
admitted that he was probably the father of the child Miss
Martin was expecting—there was no way for him to deny
it in the face of the evidence—and obviously she was his
mistress. He probably caught them at it and this caused
him to go into a murderous rage."

"Then, why didn't he kill them right then and there?"

"Too public. After all, he wasn't a complete fool. He
must have dissembled and persuaded them to accompany
him to the Greek theater, where he killed the girl first.
Somehow the big Negro escaped, but Russell caught up
with him at the amphitheater later and shot him, after first
hiding Miss Martin's body. It was a sex crime—you'll see!
No dope, no smuggling, really quite simple. Russell hasn't
confessed yet, but he will, soon enough."

"But what about the figurines and 'mammoth,' and why
were the two murdered people dressed in their acting costumes?" Toby protested. "There is so much you haven't
explained."

"All in good time." Hamit Bey waved a placating hand.
"Naturally, there are many loose ends still to be tied up,
but now that I am sure we have our man, we'll soon find
the explanation for all of these things."

"And what of the disappearance of Vincent and Mrs.
Thompson?" Toby put in. "You surely can't lay that to
Russell as well? He was right here when they disap-
peared."

"Oh, I think I can explain that," Hamit said easily.

"And it's sex again—you'll see! Vincent obviously lied about the camper. He was probably off somewhere with Mrs. Thompson and didn't realize it had been used until after he had made his statement. Now they are both scared because they lied to the police and have run off together. Stupid of them, since they have little hope of getting out of Turkey undetected, but perfectly understandable. In any case, I am expecting to hear at any moment that they have been apprehended, because that is my second bit of fortunate news: the camper has been found!" He nodded triumphantly at Toby.

"Where?"

"It was found abandoned just on the outskirts of Afyon Karahissar. I suppose they decided it was too easily spotted to take very far and either hired another car or got a plane out of Afyon to Istanbul, hoping to get away before we spot them. Some hope!"

"Afyon Karahissar—the center of the opium-growing region! And you don't find that significant?" Toby demanded.

"Not particularly. They were probably too scared to risk Izmir again, and Vincent already knew there were flights to Istanbul from Afyon from his last trip there. I know he was up there, because they had some difficulty with the *ikamet* of one of them—the old man, I seem to remember —and the local police contacted me at the time. We'll soon know for sure, since Mrs. Thompson would stick out in a crowd whatever means of transport she used, and now we know where to look. By the way, the Afyon police are having the camper driven back here by one of their men, and we'll give it a very thorough going-over this time."

He was interrupted by a loud knock on the door followed by the precipitate entrance of Bilger, who froze at the sight of Toby. However, Hamit Bey's genial mood would brook no delays. "Come on in," he boomed. "What have you got for me? Don't mind *Bay* Glendower; he's a man who I am confident knows how to guard his tongue."

Bilger reluctantly delivered his message. "The Afyon police have picked up the trail. A woman answering the description of Mrs. Thompson took the flight to Istanbul this very morning. She appeared to be traveling alone."

"Hmm. They must have split up, then." Hamit wrinkled his brow. "Has Afyon checked their car rental?"

"Yes. No one answering Vincent's description has hired a car."

"I wonder if she dropped him off somewhere and he's making for Eskisehir, planning to meet her later in Istanbul," Hamit said, a trace of uneasiness creeping into his voice.

"I thought of that, and the Eskisehir police are checking now."

"Good. All right, now I think the best thing to do is for you to get after Mrs. Thompson right away. If you hurry, you can get a plane out of Izmir today. It's best you go; you know the woman and can speak her language. Her trail should be easy enough to pick up in Istanbul. She'll have to check into one of the hotels. I'll phone ahead to Istanbul so that, with any luck, they'll have the information for you by the time you get there." Bilger turned to go, but Hamit checked him. "Oh, what about the camper?"

"It has already left Afyon and should be here later this afternoon."

Having got his machine once more smoothly into action, Hamit was all smiles. He got up. "So things march, eh, *Bay* Glendower? Now, if you will excuse me, I think I'll go and see if Mr. Russell is in a more talkative mood."

Toby rose with him. "Are my colleague and I still under the ban not to leave Bergama?" he asked slowly. "Not that we actually wish to leave, but I was thinking of hiring a car and taking a drive, maybe even taking a run into Izmir."

"I can see no harm in that," Hamit Bey said expansively. "I hope a couple of days will see this matter completely cleared up, and then you'll be free to carry on with your trip as planned."

"Oh, one other thing. Have you had any report yet on the figurines?"

There was a trace of scorn in Hamit's voice as he replied, "Ah, yes, of course you would be interested in those. I was forgetting that you are an archaeologist. Yes, I have the report here somewhere." He scrabbled among the papers on his desk. "Here it is." He did not hand it to Toby but stood reading it. "All it says is that the figurines are gold, early Hittite probably, and that the soil sample taken from one of them indicates it could have come from the Bergama region. Does that satisfy you?"

"I see," said Toby thoughtfully. "Well, thank you, thank you very much."

"Hire a car!" It was sometime later, and there was disapproval in Penny's voice as she repeated, "Hire a car! But I thought we agreed, since rental cars are so hideously expensive, we'd stick to public transport and just get taxis when we needed them."

"Nevertheless, I am going to," Toby said stubbornly. "In fact, I've already done so. I'm thinking of making some trips to Izmir, and I feel it would do us both good to get out of this place for a bit; so how about coming for a drive now?"

"Well, it's your money," Penny said with resignation. It was one of her pet phrases "All right, where shall we go?"

"Oh, just around and about," Toby answered vaguely, "just around and about."

"You certainly meant what you said," Penny remarked when they had been driving over an hour. "I swear we've been going around and around in circles. I've now seen the old city from every conceivable angle." She gasped as the car swerved dangerously near the deep ditch at the side of the road. "For God's sake, Toby, keep your eyes on the road! You'll have us both in the hospital at this rate. Your head has been on a constant swivel since we left the hotel. Are you looking for something or what? You've hardly said a word. What's on your mind?"

"Nothing definite. Just an idea," Toby muttered as his eyes continued to scan the rocky terrain.

"Well, can't you at least tell me about it?" she demanded.

"So far there is absolutely nothing to tell," he said with deepening gloom. "Had enough?"

"Quite," she said firmly. "Anyway, we'd better be getting back; it's almost dinnertime."

Toby sighed and turned the car back toward the hotel. They returned to find the assistant manager hopping up

and down nervously, with a message for Toby to return to
the police station immediately. However traumatic the
more involved inhabitants of the hotel might be finding
the current situation, it was quite evident that the young
manager had not had so much excitement in his entire life
and was thoroughly relishing every moment of it.

"I wonder what it is now," Penny said worriedly.

Toby glanced at his watch. "The camper should have
arrived from Afyon. Maybe they've turned up something in
it—perhaps even the missing weapons." He hurried off.

He was partly right. Hamit met him, his face once more
dark and concerned, and ushered him into the echoing confines of the police garage. "There's something I want you
to see," he said grimly.

The contents of the camper were piled around the floor,
and police were swarming over the body of the vehicle
like ants in the process of dismembering their prey. Costumes, cameras and assorted small props lay in separate
heaps, but Hamit led Toby to a small pile of objects that
had been set apart from the rest. "My men have been very
careless," he said tightly. "They tried to excuse themselves
by saying they were only told to look for the weapons, but
there is no excuse for such carelessness." He bent down,
picked up one of the larger, empty camera cases and, like
a disgruntled magician revealing his *tour de force,* with a
few sharp taps removed successively the bottom and two
sides of the case, exposing empty, shallow compartments
within. "All the camera cases are like this," he rasped.
"False bottoms, false sides—and some of the props that
have been made to appear solid are actually no more than
cleverly made, hollowed-out shells. Obviously, they have
all been specially made for one purpose—smuggling. It
looks as if you were right after all—drugs."

"Or small antiquities," Toby said carefully.

"Possibly. But there's bigger money in drugs; so, taking
everything else into consideration, I think they are the
most likely answer."

They looked at one another in silence for a minute;
then Hamit Bey went on. "Thompson was one of the prop-
men. He must have known. And so must Wolf Vincent. I
am extremely anxious to talk to that gentleman. He is

going to have a great deal of explaining to do—a very great deal."

Toby eyed Hamit keenly. "And you think perhaps Thompson revealed this to Melody Martin?"

"On the face of it, that certainly seems probable—thereby providing an excellent motive for the murder of them both by Thompson's accomplice or accomplices," he finished heavily.

"Yes, it explains a lot of things," Toby said, as if to himself, "but not all, by no means all. There are still the costumes, 'mammoth,' and the figurines. It all has to fit together somehow, and it still doesn't. Is there any indication of anything having been in the secret compartments recently?"

"We have not had the time for tests on them yet, but they should give some indication," the police chief answered.

"And still no sign of the weapons?"

"None."

An excited voice calling Hamit Bey was heard from within the station, and soon a constable poked his head excitedly out of the door. "Kosay on the phone for you, *effendi,* from Istanbul."

Hamit Bey strode off, Toby following determinedly behind him. The connection was evidently bad, for Hamit at once started bellowing into it for Bilger to speak louder.

The line gradually cleared, and Bilger's voice came thin and tinny over the wire. "I've got the Thompson woman, chief, and will be bringing her back on the morning plane to Izmir. There's nothing more out of here tonight."

"Vincent, what of Vincent?" Hamit shouted anxiously. "There have been some new developments here, and he must be found. Stay there if you have to, but *find* him."

"That's just it, Hamit Bey. The Thompson woman swears he never left Bergama. She says he gave her the camper and some money and told her to go. Then, when I told her he was missing, she shut up like a clam. Says she won't say another word until she has talked to Dr. Spring."

"What the— What's *she* got to do with it?" yelled Hamit angrily. "And where's Vincent?"

"I don't know, chief. All I know is that Gale Thompson

said he had her drive him a little outside of town, and then she let him off and didn't see him again."

"Where did she leave him and when?"

"She said it was just before that violent storm broke the other night—at the Greek theater on the acropolis."

CHAPTER 10

"I guess my idea wasn't such a good one after all. Am I in big trouble, Dr. Spring? Can you help me?" The dark girl's eyes pleaded with Penny, who stood looking worriedly down at her.

"Yes, I'm afraid you were extremely foolish to go off like that, Gale. The best thing for you to do now is to tell me everything that happened between the time we last spoke and now—particularly about Wolf Vincent."

There had been an almighty hassle after Bilger returned with the sullenly uncommunicative girl in tow. Hamit Bey had been furious at Gale's insistence on talking with Penny before she made a statement of any sort to the police. He had been persuaded only after the greatest of difficulty to allow Penny to see Gale unhampered by the presence of a policeman.

Gale shook her head wretchedly from side to side. "But won't that only make things worse? The last thing I want is to get Wolf into trouble—he's been so decent to me."

"No. You've *got* to tell me everything; don't hold anything back now. And you've also got to realize I'll have to pass it all on to the police. It's a small miracle, as it is, that they've allowed me to see you alone like this. I dare not hold anything back from them. Also, it is most vital that Wolf be found."

The dark eyes clouded. "Yes, I don't understand that—not at all," Gale said in a worried tone, "From what he said, I thought he'd be doing this one last thing and then going back to the hotel for Carla and getting out, himself."

"Look," Penny said patiently, "just take it one step at a time. Starting the story in midstream is only going to confuse us both. Tell me what happened from when you left me that day on the road." She sat down next to Gale and patted her hand.

Gale looked at her with troubled eyes. "It goes back before then. I was just trying to tell you that day that I meant to go away. I knew Wolf was going to help me, but I still didn't know how. You remember that first day we met and Wolf took me aside? Well, it was then he said he didn't like the way things were going, that he thought I'd be safer away from here and would do all he could to help me. I didn't know how he planned to do that, and I think he didn't, either. He kept probing me about what Washington had said the last few days we were together, but there was little I could tell him. He got quite angry with me at one point. I think he thought I was holding out on him for some reason, but it wasn't so. It just wasn't!"

She was becoming agitated; so Penny said soothingly. "All right now, don't get upset. What happened the day you left?"

"Well, you remember Wolf had taken me to look for the daggers in the camper? He kept asking me if I knew of any hidden place they might be, and I told him no. Then he seemed to make up his mind about something and said to hang in there and he'd get me away.

"After I went for the walk with you that day, I found him waiting for me in my room. He gave me a thousand dollars. I've no idea where he got that much, but, anyway, there it was. He said it wasn't enough to get me to Sydney but more than enough to get me back to France, and he gave me the name of a man in Marseilles who he said would give me the rest of the money I needed to buy the ticket to Australia. He told me to go back home as fast as I could and 'get lost.' He said that the authorities here wouldn't go to all the trouble and expense of trying to find me out there, because I hadn't done anything." She swallowed hard. "I asked him if he was coming, too, but he didn't seem to like the question. First of all, he said he couldn't leave Carla in the lurch like that, however bad things were between them." Penny felt a quickening sense of excitement. "And then he said he had some things to take care of, that he couldn't let 'it' go on any longer. He never said what 'it' was, but that he and Carla would not be far behind me."

"And what about the camper?" Penny queried. "Why, if

you had the money for it, didn't you just hire a car and go into Izmir and get a plane? You must have known the camper, being as outstanding as it is in this country, would be easily traced and spotted."

Gale hesitated before replying. "Well, it was what he asked me to do," she said reluctantly. "In the first place, he wanted me to take him up to the old Greek theater, and he did not want to be seen going there. I had an idea there was something there he either wanted to find or find out about—he wouldn't say—and in the second place, he wanted the camper out of the way. He said Izmir would be too dangerous to leave from, being so near and the first place they'd look, and told me exactly how to get to Afyon. He even had a schedule of flight times from Afyon airport."

"But didn't he realize that even if you got away, the camper would be found and brought back? I mean, I just don't see the point of it all," Penny said confusedly.

Again Gale hesitated, and it was evident she was having quite a struggle with herself about something. "But it wasn't meant to be found," she said finally in a whisper. "You see, he told me to get rid of it—even showed me how, with rags and some tins of gasoline, and said it had to be burned to cover my traces. He told me to ditch it in some quiet spot outside of Afyon and burn it."

"Why didn't you do as he said, then?" Penny said sharply.

Gale looked at her with troubled eyes. "Because I couldn't see any point to it. I mean, I've got nothing really against Scrowski Productions. To me it seemed a senseless piece of vandalism to burn all their equipment and that expensive truck. I thought Wolf was getting back at them a bit unfairly—though I understood why—and, well, I just didn't want to be a party to it. Also, when I got to Afyon, I couldn't really find anywhere hidden enough so that a big blaze like that wouldn't have been noticed immediately. So I figured if I left it in a secluded spot, it would still give Wolf time to do whatever he had to do and get away before it was found."

"Are you in love with him?" Penny queried.

Gale shook her head hopelessly. "I know this is difficult

to believe, but, no, there was nothing like that between Wolf and me. Oh, I admit I did my damnedest to give that impression at times. Partly it was to try and wake Washington up a bit; let's face it, Wolf is a very attractive man. But, no, he wasn't even remotely interested in me for that reason." She paused. "I think you can understand this better than anyone, Dr. Spring. There is a strong bond between us because we are both making our way in a white man's world. I've made a success of it and so has he, and it really is the most important thing in his life. He's a militant for his own people and all other minority groups. His camerawork is just a way to make a living, good as he is at it, but it's the cause that means everything to him. The Vincents are poor because practically everything he makes goes back into the cause."

"In that case," Penny said bluntly, "why does he hang on to Angus McLean's coattails—Angus is white. And, for that matter, why does he work for a rather third-rate outfit? He could make more money and do more for his cause—if it's so important to him—elsewhere."

For the first time a faint grin appeared on Gale's face. "I see you haven't talked very much with Angus yet," she said. "According to him, he belongs to one of the most oppressed minorities in the world—the Celts! He is a declared militant; there is a very strong bond on that score between him and Wolf, who feels he has suffered great injustice because of his political beliefs."

"And yet they are both prepared to work for a dynastic capitalist like Scrowski," Penny observed wryly.

"Scrowski at least had guts enough to buck the system to hire Angus when no one else would," Gale retorted with some heat.

"And got himself a bargain package," Penny murmured. She was not in the least impressed by this "all for the cause and the world well lost" theme that Gale was developing, since the evidence was beginning to point so clearly in more mercenary directions.

"Anyway," Gale muttered sulkily, "I've answered your question. There wasn't anything going on between Wolf and me."

"So let's get back to what happened," Penny said

equably. "He asked you to take him to the theater, burn the camper and take a plane from Afyon. What else did he tell you to do?"

"It all happened so fast," Gale complained, wrinkling her brows. "It's hard to remember everything. Before we left that day, he told me to take just one suitcase and to leave the rest of my things—anything I didn't care about —so that if they looked in my room, it would not be immediately clear I'd gone off. So I just threw a few things in my bag and we sneaked out the back way. Then, when we got to the camper, something seemed to strike him. He stood looking around him for a minute, and it was then that he asked me to drive him out to the Greek theater. He hadn't mentioned it before."

"Have you any idea what it was?" Penny asked.

Gale shook her head.

A sudden thought struck Penny. "How about the cars? Were all the cars there?"

Gale reflected. "I seem to recall the sedan was in the parking lot, but I don't remember the jeep. No, I think the jeep definitely was not there."

"Do you recall the time?"

Again Gale shook her head. "No, I'm afraid not."

"Had the storm begun?"

"No. That I do remember. I had taken Wolf up to the theater and was on the main road making for the turnoff for Afyon when it broke. I remember being thankful I was off that narrow track, because it would have turned to mud in an instant in a downpour such as that was. It was all I could do to keep the camper going even on the tarmac. The rain was coming down in such sheets the wipers didn't help much."

"And where exactly did you leave him?"

"I dropped him off at that tunnel, and he went straight in. I had such a job turning the camper—I'm not a good driver, and that's a heavy machine to operate—that I was tempted to go in after him and ask him to come and give me a hand with it. Then I looked up and saw him outlined against the sky right at the top of the theater; so I somehow managed by myself."

"And that was the last you saw of him? What was he doing?"

Gale nodded. "He was just looking out over the rest of the ruins—up the hill."

"And there was no sign of anyone else?"

"No one."

"What do you think became of him?" Penny said.

Gale's face crumpled. "I've no idea," she whispered. "But, oh, God, I hope nothing has happened to him! He was only trying to help me, that I swear!"

Penny was silent for a moment. "And what was the trouble between him and his wife? There *was* trouble, wasn't there?"

The eyes became veiled and hard. "Why don't you ask Carla that? Wolf never discussed their private affairs with me."

Penny decided there was no use pressing this obviously unwelcome topic. "Did he give you any advice about what to do after you got out of Afyon?"

Gale seemed relieved at the change of subject. "Yes. He didn't know about international flights out of Istanbul, but he said if I was lucky, maybe there'd be one the same day. If not, he told me to stay in a hotel overnight on the old side of the city—near the sultan's palace and the old covered market—and not to go to the European section, where the police would look first if they tumbled to the fact I'd gone."

"Did he say any particular hotel?"

"Yes, the Ozipek Palas; he even wrote it down for me. It was a terribly run-down old place."

Penny looked at her thoughtfully. "And how did he know about it? He'd never stayed in Istanbul, had he?"

Gale shrugged. "He may have—I just don't know. All he knew was the name, I think. He couldn't tell me how to get there, and I had quite a time finding it. Not that it made much difference—they tracked me down anyway." She sighed heavily. "I never would have thought they could be so efficient. I wonder how they got on to everything so quickly."

"Well, for one thing, Carla gave the alarm not more than a couple of hours after you left," Penny said drily. "It's a wonder you even got as far as Istanbul without being picked up. They found the camper not long after you'd left Afyon, and from there it was easy to trace you."

Again Gale sighed heavily. "I suppose I should have burned it just as Wolf told me to."

"I'm very glad you didn't. You're in enough trouble as it is," Penny said. "It would be much worse if you had destroyed vital evidence."

"What evidence? You mean the murder weapons were in there after all?"

Penny looked at her keenly. "You really don't know, do you? Probably it's better that you shouldn't. Luckily, just at the moment, the police are far more interested in finding Wolf than in throwing the book at you—or, at least, I hope so. You realize that I'll have to tell them everything you've told me?"

"Do you have to tell them everything?" Gale murmured. "I mean about burning the camper? Surely that will be awfully bad for Wolf when the rest hear of it, particularly that De Witt bitch."

"I'll certainly have to tell the police, but there's no reason the rest of the company need know," Penny assured her. "I'll do the best I can to cool the police down, but Hamit Bey is not the most reasonable of men, particularly where women are concerned; so you may have to stay here overnight. Toby plans to go into Izmir tomorrow to contact the Australian consul, if there is one; if not, the British. You ought to have someone official helping you with this, and since you're still an Australian citizen, they'd be the ones to do it. Now, you're certain you've told me everything—you're not holding anything back?"

"Everything I can think of," Gale said sadly. "I can't say how thankful I am you're here, Dr. Spring. I guess I'd really be up the creek if it weren't for you."

"Well, just don't lose your courage; I'm sure we'll get you out of this," Penny said with far more conviction than she felt.

The ensuing two hours were every bit as difficult as she had anticipated and left her both drained and defeated. She related Gale's story to an audience of Bilger, the chief and Toby, who all listened in a grim, stony silence. At the end of her narration, Bilger asked, "And would you say she was telling the truth?"

"About the main events, I would be willing to swear she was," Penny said firmly. "The only reservation I have is about her feelings for Wolf Vincent, which I think may be deeper than she has stated, or perhaps is willing to admit even to herself."

"And she is now prepared to make a sworn statement?"

"Yes."

"It certainly alters the picture," Hamit Bey said in an aside to Toby. Then he continued to Bilger: "Well, there are certain things that must be taken care of immediately. A warrant of arrest must be issued for Wolf Vincent, and a full-scale search mounted for him. Istanbul police must be contacted for any information they have on that hotel, the name and address of the man in Marseilles checked with Interpol. It is evident that Wolf Vincent, if indeed he is not the mainspring, was deeply involved in the smuggling. His anxiety to destroy the camper proves that. We may try checking the money he gave to Mrs. Thompson, as well; it is possible we may be able to track it down to her husband."

"You think Vincent took it from Thompson after he killed him?"

"It looks like it. We know Thompson had a big wad of it at nine-forty-five A.M. on the day he was killed, and none was found on him. Yes, practically everything fits now."

"But not the figurines or the costumes or 'mammoth,'" Toby murmured stubbornly.

Hamit brushed this aside with a wave of his hand.

"And Russell?"

Hamit Bey admitted grudgingly that in the light of the new evidence he would be released from custody, at least for the moment. But when Penny entered a similar plea for Gale, she was turned down with an adamant no.

Toby tried to add his plea to hers but was turned upon by Hamit Bey. "You have repeatedly expressed anxiety over Mrs. Thompson's safety. We are holding her as a material witness; we're not charging her with anything, at least for now. Where could she be safer than in our custody?"

Toby fell back on his second line of defense. "Then,

if you hold her, I shall be forced to notify the Australian consul, and you'll have to answer to him."

"There's no Australian consul in Izmir," Hamit informed him.

"Well, then, the British consul, who, in that case, would handle these matters," Toby said stiffly.

"Do that." Hamit smirked at him strangely. "I have already been through this with Mr. McLean, who seems as anxious as you are to keep Mrs. Thompson out of our hands, only in his case he threatened me with the American consul. I gave him the same answer I am giving you. We intend to hold Mrs. Thompson until Wolf Vincent is located and charged."

There did not seem much point in continuing the argument after that; so Toby and Penny took their leave, passing on their way the woebegone figure of Gale being escorted in. Penny stopped for a hasty word with her, under the suspicious stares of her escort. "Look, dear," she said hurriedly, "they are going to keep you here for the moment because it's safer. Now, don't worry. Toby Glendower is going to see the British consul on your behalf first thing tomorrow; so just be patient." Gale nodded sadly and was gone.

When Penny rejoined Toby, she found Brett Russell with him and was taken aback at the sight, for in the two days of his incarceration he had aged by twenty years. When she first saw him in the hotel, she had thought how well preserved he was, his face under the neat beard still maintaining the clean lines she remembered from his matinee-idol youth, his virile figure still slim and agile. Now he was stooped and shriveled, the flesh of his face sagging beneath the beard that was uncombed and scrofulous, and there were heavy pouches beneath the fine dark eyes. Even his movements had lost their elasticity and certainty as he silently followed them out of the police station.

Once outside, he stopped and breathed deeply of the fresh night air, gazing upward at the star-filled sky. "Oh, God, you don't know how good that looks," he said. He turned to Toby. "I understand I owe you my thanks for this release, Dr. Glendower. That English-speaking policeman told me just now how you've been championing my cause since they first started to question me. I do not know how to begin to thank you."

Toby squirmed with embarrassment. "I did very little, I'm afraid. I just tried to point out how weak the case was against you. I never believed you to be involved at all."

Brett Russell stood there in the darkness, silent for a moment; then he said, "I wonder if you'd come and have a drink with me somewhere? I don't feel like going back to the hotel just yet or facing the rest of them. Since you've done this for me and have taken such a deep interest in what's been happening, I'd like to tell you my side of it."

"Well, Dr. Spring has had a rather exhausting time of it; so perhaps—" Toby was silenced by a quick kick on the shin by Penny, who was dying to hear what Russell had to say about Melody.

She said quickly to cover up Toby's sharp yip of pain, "Why we'd love to, Mr. Russell."

After some hunting around to find a place that was still open, they finally were settled at a small table in a drab, neon-lit bar. Rather grubby thick glasses full of a dubious-looking brandy stood in front of them. To Brett Russell, however, the alcohol was such a welcome sight that he downed two in rapid succession before he started to unburden himself. The brandy brought some color back into his ashen face, but his hands still shook as he grasped his third drink. He gazed into it reflectively, then glanced up at them. "I suppose they told you I've admitted that I was the father of Melody's child?"

Toby nodded. Brett sighed and said, "And yet it wasn't a bit like they made it sound, you know, not a bit. I don't know if I can get you to understand about Melody—I'm not sure I understand myself. She was a very unusual girl, you know. I've never seen anyone who had quite such an urge to be needed—needed more than loved, I think—and she was prepared to go to any lengths for it."

"Including blackmail?" Toby queried gently.

"Well, yes and no," Brett said in a puzzled tone. "It depends what you mean by blackmail. About this child, for instance—no, I can't start there. I'll have to go back a bit further." He looked appealingly at them. "I'm afraid

I'm not too good at explaining things. Melody and I had a thing going for about two months, you know. I'd heard she was an easy lay—apart from Scrowski, I knew of several others—and, well, she was very lovely with those gorgeous legs and those beautiful blue eyes." Toby and Penny exchanged a quick glance. "I mean, a real dream girl, you know. I was never serious, but, for that matter, neither was she. We both got what we wanted out of it, and while it was on, it was all very pleasant—apart from her endless curiosity. She was always asking questions. I'd had a wife like that once, and I found it doesn't pay to say too much, you know; so she didn't get a lot out of me. Then she sprang it on me that she was pregnant and I was 'daddy.' I did all the right things. I offered to pay for an abortion and so on, you know, but she staggered me a bit by saying she wanted the baby and was going to have it. I scented the old black right there and laid it on the line. I said if she was thinking to queer this thing I had going with a very fine lady—whose name I won't mention—to forget it, it wouldn't work, and she knew already I had no money to speak of. She acted quite hurt, said she had no intention of strong-arming me. I told her if she was planning to pull a Barry/Chaplin act after the kid was born, she could forget that, too, you know. She laughed at me and said I didn't understand her at all; she even put it in writing that she would make no claims on me for the child. I've got the statement in a safe-deposit box back in the States." He looked sheepishly at Penny. "That may seem a bit hard, but I've had quite a bit of experience with women, you know—some of it unfortunate—and I've learned to be careful."

"Did she say why she wanted the child?" Penny asked.

"Well, nothing that made any sense to me," Brett said simply. "Something about how it would be a part of me that only she knew about, and that it might be nice for me to know I had a child growing up somewhere, like some of the other stars have." He looked almost coy. "And she said having a child if you weren't married these days was almost a status symbol in Hollywood, showed you were really liberated and could go it alone—only no one was ever really alone, you know, because everyone was needed—" He stopped in some confusion, as if the muddled thoughts were too much for him.

"And then?" Toby prompted.

"Then? Nothing. We were just good friends. She didn't mention it again, and when she went off for a few days, I thought maybe she'd ditched the kid after all. She was playing up to some of the other members of the company by that time."

"And you weren't jealous?"

Russell looked astonished. "No—a bit relieved, to be truthful." He gave a world-weary sigh. "These action films take a lot more out of me than they used to, and I can do without these hot, heavy entanglements on the side, you know. Also, of course, I hope to get married again at the end of this film. I may even retire." He sounded hopeful.

"Was there anyone in particular Melody was involved with at the time of her death?"

Brett shrugged. "I wouldn't say so. She'd given a tumble in the hay to young Andrew, I think—to judge by the way Carla Vincent was acting up—and she'd been making time with that big black lout, and I think she'd even had a go with Vincent, but she wasn't in one of her hot spells—I could tell that. Seemed to me she was up to something, but I don't know what."

"Then, have you any idea who killed her?"

Brett wrinkled his brow. "Well, it wasn't me. They kept digging me at the station that it was a sex crime, you know. I can't see it that way, but if it was, I'd plunk for the buck nigger. She may have led him on, you know, and then wouldn't come across. She was a bit of a racist," he added naïvely. He swallowed the last of his drink and, leaning back, treated them to one of his "send 'em swooning" supersmiles. "I feel much better now that I've told you everything, just so you understand how it really was, you know. Now I'd better get back and get some shuteye—I'm beat. Got to get the old face back in shape for when the cameras start rolling again. I wonder who Scrowski will put in Melody's part."

Toby and Penny looked at him in blank amazement.

"You don't mean you think the picture will go on after all this, do you?" Penny said weakly.

Brett looked utterly astonished, "Why of course! You don't think Hy Scrowski is going to let a mammoth tax write-off like this go down the drain do you? What do you think this was all about, anyhow? This was just one of Hy's jokes on the taxmen, you know!"

CHAPTER 11

Toby decapitated an egg, peered dubiously into its runny interior and said with a sigh, "I don't know about you, but I must say I find these people infernally hard to come to grips with. I mean, what did you make of that fellow last night and all that business about the film at the end?"

"Well, they do have a very different way of looking at things," Penny said with caution. "Sort of Alice-in-Wonderlandish from our point of view, but neither of us understands the first thing about movies or big business. My mind boggles at the thought of pouring thousands of dollars into a movie that's not meant to make any money, but, then, I've never had thousands of dollars to play with."

"He did use the word *mammoth*, you notice," Toby said.

"I think that was just a figure of speech, you know—oh, damn! I'm beginning to catch that wretched habit. I thought last night I'd scream if he said it one more time."

"That's curious, too, I found," Toby ruminated. "Practically every student these days has that ghastly verbal tic, but a man of Russell's age?"

"As far as mental age goes, I'd put him down as a retarded adolescent," Penny said caustically. "All on the outside, nothing in."

"Mmm," agreed Toby and pushed aside his abandoned egg with a discouraged sigh. "I'd better be under way. No one who knew anything was at the damned consulate when I phoned; so I'll have to go on spec. Want to come?"

"No, I don't think so. I'm going to see Gale again, if they'll let me. Also, I'd probably be more profitably employed doing some snooping around here."

"No more careening off over the countryside looking

for Wolf Vincent with your Turkish friend, mind!" Toby said with some anxiety.

"I wasn't planning to, but why not, pray tell?"

"Because you may be in some danger—I've told you that before. The murderer might think you know more than you've been saying."

"I should think he would be over the hills and far away by now, not lurking around here to polish me off."

"You mean, you think Vincent is the murderer?" said Toby with surprise.

"Why, yes. It certainly looks like it. Don't you think so? Everything fits in."

"No, not everything." Toby shook his head worriedly. "I have a feeling it is far more complicated than that."

"A *feeling!*" echoed Penny with asperity. "That's all we need now, for you to go into one of your 'fey' spells. At the rate you're going, we'll soon have everyone in the film company incapable of committing the murders, and we'll be right back where we started. We'll *never* get out of here. In any case, to put your mind at rest, I assure you I have no intention of going off anywhere. So run along and see if you can bring back the weight of the British empire behind you to rescue poor Gale."

Several hours later Toby was reflecting gloomily that he knew exactly why the British empire had crumbled so far and so fast and that one of the principal reasons was embodied in the man now sitting across the desk from him, being blandly unhelpful. It had not improved Toby's temper to have been left cooling his heels for an hour and a half before the consul put in an appearance. And although the latter had professed "pressing business" as an excuse, his pink straight-from-the-bath look and freshly shaved chubby jowls, plus the almost overpowering aroma of one of the most chic men's after-shave lotions, indicated that Her Majesty's consul had just belatedly arisen.

The consul had struck a wrong note at the very outset when, after consulting Toby's proferred card, he giggled in a rather shrill falsetto and announced himself to be from "the other place." "Trinity, Cambridge, actually, from Harrow," he said, fingering his old Harrovian tie to emphasize his point. Toby (Winchester College and Magdalen, Oxford) was unimpressed. The consul then compounded his error. "I believe congratulations are in order, are they not? Didn't I see your name on the last honors list? *Sir* Tobias, eh? Amazing how you archaeology chaps always seem to end up with knighthoods, while we poor civil servants are lucky to end up with an O.B.E. these days!" There followed a seemingly endless series of "Do you know old so-and-so," which Toby sullenly and emphatically answered in the negative, thereby denying some of his closest associates and friends. Finally, having run out of names to drop, the consul got around to the inevitable question: "Well, what can I do for you, Sir Tobias?"

"It hasn't happened yet," snapped Toby testily, "so please, Bullstrode-Smith, just Glendower!"

"Bullstrode-*Smythe*," he was corrected.

"Whatever! And I hope you can do quite a lot for me. It's about this very nasty business in Bergama."

"What nasty business?" the consul said blankly.

It was Toby's turn to be surprised. "You haven't heard from Angus McLean about the murders in his film company?"

"Angus McLean!" Bullstrode-Smythe brushed his hand nervously over the thinning hair on the crown of his head. "You mean the Communist film director? The one the Americans kicked out?" Again he sniggered nervously. "Thought he was dead. What's he doing here, and what's all this about murders?"

"Obviously he *hasn't* been in touch with you yet," Toby said grimly, "but he will be, since there are several British nationals involved, myself included." He gave in terse outline the sequence of events, punctuated at regular intervals by "Good Lord!" from the now officially-concerned-looking consul.

At the end of Toby's recital, the consul said brightly, "So you want me to get you out of this mess, eh? No problem. I'll just get on the line to Ankara, and the embassy will have you out of there in a jiffy." He reached for the phone.

Toby held up a restraining hand. "No—wait! I'm not here for myself—it's for an Australian girl in the film company whom the Turkish police have in custody at the moment. I believe that in the absence of the Australians, the British take jurisdiction in cases like this."

"Oh, like that, is it?" A slight smirk appeared on the consul's small, fleshy mouth, and his hand strayed to the knot of his tie. "Dashed attractive some of those Aussie girls, if you can overlook that frightful accent—what!"

"This is an Australian girl who met the boat," Toby said with heavy irony.

"Met the boat? Sorry, but I don't follow you, old man."

"She's an Australian aborigine."

"You mean a *black* Aussy?" The hand dropped away from the tie and commenced a nervous tattoo on the desk.

Toby seized the opportunity to sketch out Gale's current plight. The consul listened with a deepening frown. At the end Toby said, "I was hoping you would return with me to Bergama and persuade the chief of police to at least leave her at liberty under your cognizance until the matter is cleared up. It must be very unpleasant for a young woman in a Turkish jail, and I am convinced she is not directly concerned in the murders."

Bullstrode-Smythe cleared his throat nervously. "I'm afraid that's out of the question. Not actually our affair at all, y'know. Best I can do is to pass the message on to the embassy and get them to contact the nearest Aussies. A messy affair like this we couldn't get directly involved in. Up to her people, y'know . . ." he trailed off.

"So you won't help?" Toby said waspishly.

"Not won't, *can't*, Glendower, old chap." The consul had recovered his urbanity. "You might have a go at the American consul—you say the girl was married to a Yank? They may have some jurisdiction, and you know how they are for getting involved in absolutely everything!"

"No, I know nothing of the sort," Toby snapped. Then, realizing it would do no good to antagonize the man, he went on more equably. "How and where do I get in touch with him?"

"Ah! That might present some difficulty," the consul said with ill-concealed malice. "He's always off junketing somewhere, but, if you're in luck, you may catch him on one of his breathing spells in the office." He got up to signal the end of the interview.

Toby reluctantly rose, too. "You *will* get on to Ankara directly about Mrs. Thompson?" he demanded.

"Oh, of course." But Bullstrode-Smythe made no move toward the phone. Instead he stuck out his hand and gave Toby a limp handshake, "And if there is anything I can do for *you*, please let me know."

Mentally cursing petty bureaucrats in general and English snobs in particular, Toby went off in search of the American consul, only to find that—as had been predicted —he was away from the consulate and would not be available until the following day. The best Toby could do was to make a firm appointment to see him at ten-thirty the next morning.

After some debate with himself, he decided to skip lunch and made for the Izmir museum, where—after he had identified himself—he had a long and highly technical talk with the director about the Hittite gold figurines and was rewarded with a couple bits of information that added fuel to the fire of suspicion that had been steadily growing in him.

The figurines from Melody's handbag had been the first in gold of that type seen, but there had been others in bronze that had appeared in the Izmir antique market and which the museum had acquired. The director showed them to Toby. "Granted, the obvious thought would be that they've been brought in from Hittite country, but that doesn't make too much sense. They'd get more for them *in* Hittite country, if you see what I mean. Not so much doubt as to their authenticity. Also, we've had a couple of Hittite pots—early type, too, about the same era. I'd swear they didn't come from very far away."

"To get a Hittite settlement out this far in the southwest would be a bit unlikely," Toby observed.

"Yes. I doubt that very much. I was thinking more of a tomb. All the things so far would fit in well enough with burial goods."

"But isn't that even more unlikely?"

The director shrugged unhappily. "It's just an idea of mine—maybe a crazy one—but Hittite princesses married outside of their own area. I suppose it is possible that one got sent this far."

"The tomb of a Hittite princess—that's quite an idea!" Toby rumbled and took his leave deep in thought.

It was still rather early; so he decided to check the two hotels the company had stayed in on the night prior to the murders, in the faint hope of unearthing some overlooked nugget of information.

The manager of the first and less luxurious of the two, patronized by McLean, White, young Andrew and the Vincents, was anxious to help but could come up with nothing new. The manager of the second, where the rest of the company had stayed, was acrimoniously unhelpful. "Film companies!" he fumed and almost spat. "They are always the same—wanting cut rates and all sorts of extras, and as unreliable as they come—showing up late or not at all—and then always trouble about the bills! And now I am saddled with all this police bother that comes after them!" he snorted in disgust.

Toby quickly picked up the point. "You mean there was someone in the company who did not use his room and then refused to pay?" he demanded.

The manager's dark eyes snapped with anger. "Yes, indeed." He fumbled through a card file with trembling fingers. "Hyman Scrowski and friend. The best suite reserved, mind you, and they would not pay!"

Toby almost snatched the card from his hand. "You mean, he was here!" he exclaimed. The reservation was dated for the day before the rest of the company arrived.

The manager shook his head. "No—he never came, and when I try to claim from that old witch, she say, 'No, no use, no pay.' *Vallah billah!*" He snatched the card back. "And I waste no further time on them or you; so be off!"

Toby's last stop was at the cab company from which Melody Martin had hired the car for the ill-fated drive to Bergama. After dispensing a liberal amount of baksheesh, Toby finally caught up with the actual driver of the car. The driver, alerted *sotto voce* by his mates that a big spender had arrived, was only too anxious to oblige, but while Toby took him painstakingly through the whole trip again, he could come up with no added detail beyond what Toby had learned already from the police. At the end Toby was struck by an inspired thought. "Tell me—for I know what fine memories you Turks have," he said carefully, "can you close your eyes and concentrate your thoughts and tell me what other vehicles were in the parking lot behind the hotel when you saw the girl and the Negro go into the big van?"

The cabdriver grinned delightedly at him and then closed his eyes. After a minute he said, "There were two other cars—a black sedan and a green convertible." He went on to describe them in greater detail; one was undoubtedly the film company's rental car.

"And that was all?" Toby asked, a shade of disappointment in his voice.

The cabdriver's face fell. "Yes," he said, his hopes of a bountiful tip fading fast, then added, "that is, if you don't count the jeep that came in while I was pulling out."

"A jeep!" Toby almost shouted with excitement. "With two men in it?"

The driver thought again and shook his head. "Only one man—of that I am positive."

"Can you describe him? Think hard."

The man screwed up his face with effort but finally shook his head. "I'm sorry, *effendi*," he confessed. "Me, I only look at cars and sometimes pretty girls. But drivers"—he shrugged—"I can tell you it was a man, but that is all."

"Well, thank you, thank you very much!" Toby said, pumping the man's hand effusively and pressing into it a tip that exceeded the driver's fondest hopes.

By now the afternoon shadows were lengthening; so Toby turned the car toward Bergama and threaded his way through the congested streets of an Izmir wakening to its evening life. He drove rapidly, sorting out the harvest of his day's work. In retrospect it had been so rich in new information that when he got to his hotel, he decided against going in. He had not finished his process of mental digestion and also was not as yet prepared to face Penny with the news of his complete failure as far as Gale was concerned.

Without really thinking, he drove in the direction of the old city and then took the dirt road up past the Greek theater, until it faded away among the ruins of the high acropolis. He got out for a stretch and then decided to have a quiet contemplative pipe among the ruins. His meanderings took him to the northern edge of the acropolis, once the site of the royal gardens. He stood at the top of the steep escarpment, gazing absentmindedly out over the rugged, rocky terrain that so suddenly humped up into saw-toothed mountains, edging the high plateau beyond. It was as desolate and as arid as a moon crater, he was thinking, when a flicker of movement below and almost directly in front of him caught his eye. It came from a long gulley running parallel to the unseen valley road, which he knew lay to his left, and its source was human, not animal. A two-legged creature was coming in one devil of a hurry through the rocky scree of the gulley, but, strain as he might, he could not make out if it was male or female, native or foreign. Cursing his own near-sightedness, Toby made a mental picture of the general contours of the gulley: a flash of pink on the left—that would be a Judas tree coming into blossom; a contorted ancient olive on the right. Snap, went the camera in his mind. It would be enough for him to identify it again.

He turned to concentrate on the running figure, which continued its stumbling, erratic path out of the gulley, then sheered off suddenly to the left, as if making for the unseen highroad.

He hesitated for a moment, wondering whether he should rush back to the car and try to meet up with whoever it was on the road, but realized at once that the person would be long gone by the time he reached that point. Instead he decided to investigate the gulley to see what had inspired such precipitate flight. Keeping his objective firmly in his mind's eye, he began a gingerly descent of the goat path that wound down from the high point of the acropolis escarpment to the barren valley below.

He arrived at the bottom completely out of breath and covered with dirt, since his expertise had not matched the goats' in the steep descent, and looked around for the gulley entrance. From this low point it was much more difficult to make out which one it was, and it was only after a couple of false starts that he came upon the Judas tree and the gnarled olive.

He started up the gulley, scanning the ground anxiously for traces of the fugitive, but the rocky scree was blankly unhelpful and treacherous underfoot, so that a lot of his attention was focused on keeping his footing. The gulley got progressively narrower and more tortuous, and he was just on the point of giving the whole thing up when he rounded a corner and the gulley suddenly opened out into a microcosmic valley in which there were some stunted shrubs and even some withered grass. Lying face-down on the grass, and attended by a sickening cloud of flies, was the body of a man.

Toby stopped, gulped and, fighting down a wave of nausea, advanced toward the body. He did not need a second glance to know what had become of Wolf Vincent.

The tall body of the Indian lay sprawled out in an unnatural position—legs and arms fully extended. In his back were two neat holes surrounded by small circles of dried blood.

Toby knelt and felt the body. It was stone cold and completely flaccid. Steeling himself, he turned it over and flinched. The handsome Indian was no longer handsome, and where the dark eyes had been were now merely sockets of putrescent ugliness. The bullets that had made such neat entrance wounds in the back had left great jagged holes in the front, ringed now by large areas of black blood and tattered clothing. It had evidently been some time since Vincent had met his unpleasant end.

When the feeling of faintness and nausea had passed and his mind started to operate again, Toby noticed two things in rapid succession. The grass he was kneeling on was still quite damp from the torrential rains of the late thunderstorm, and yet the clothing on the body both front and back was completely dry. Also, there was not the slightest vestige of blood on the damp grass. Wherever Vincent had met his end, it certainly was not here. The body had been moved.

Toby turned the body back into its original position and, standing up, could just make out a faint trail on the grass. The shoes and the lower legs of the dead man were coated with dirt and mud; so he obviously had been dragged to his present resting place. And, what was more, he had been dragged by a person of no great physical strength; so Toby concluded that, in all probability, he could not have been dragged far.

With set lips Toby started to follow the faint trail

on the grass, but luck was not with him. The grass soon gave out, to be replaced once again by the rocky scree, and by now the light was fading so fast that it was impossible to make anything out. He decided to stop and go for help. Carefully marking the furthermost point in the trail, he made his way as fast as he could in the deepening dusk out of the gulley and back up the hair-raising path to the acropolis.

He flung himself into the car and hurtled at a crazy speed down the steep road and back into Bergama, screamed up to the police station and raced inside. Brushing aside the startled protests of the constables on duty, he rushed on and into Hamit Bey's office. "I've found Vincent," he gasped, "murdered—just like the other two. And I think I may have seen the murderer. If we act quickly, we may clear this thing up tonight."

The chief was sitting quietly behind his desk in a pool of yellow lamplight, his face in shadow. He leaned forward into the light, and his glance, as he took in Toby's dirty and disheveled state, was more amused than concerned. "Bravo!" he said with a faint grin. "You have saved us a lot of trouble, *Bay* Glendower. So you have found Vincent for us."

"Well!" yelled Toby. "Aren't you coming? You act as if it is no surprise. What is this? Don't you *want* to catch the murderer?"

Hamit looked blandly at him, his dark brow furrowing. "I will be most interested to hear how you found Wolf Vincent's body, though I confess it is now no surprise to me that he is dead. However, I very much doubt you saw his murderer, *Bay* Glendower." His tone became triumphant. "You see, we already have the murderer under lock and key, and have had for the past several hours. We caught him red-handed!"

CHAPTER 12

Penny knew from the minute she left the police station that she was in for another bad day. She had failed to get past even the outer ring of constables. There was no sign of Bilger, and not even the chief was around to appeal to; of Gale she could obtain neither sight, sound nor news. Baffled, she retreated.

On her return to the hotel, her luck was no better. The only people visible were Brett Russell and Gloria, and Penny was not particularly anxious to talk to either of them. A discreet tapping on Carla Vincent's door brought no answer. Since the news of her husband's disappearance had been broadcast, both Carla and Andrew Dale had been very little in evidence, but when seen were invariably together and talking in low, serious voices. Penny would have dearly loved to know about what.

For lack of anything better to do, she went over to the letter boxes and studied them idly. There were several letters for Gloria, one for Angus McLean with a Marseilles postmark, and a couple for Josh White, one of them in bright-green ink and a sprawling feminine hand. She was just standing there wondering how Toby was faring, when a voice directly behind her made her jump. "Anything of interest to you there, Dr. Spring?" She wheeled around to find Josh grinning at her, but his eyes under the bushy brows were hard and unsmiling. He reached past her and gathered up his letters. "Still playing detective? Sort of redundant now, isn't it?" He glanced at the letters and put them into his pocket unopened. "Where's Toby got to?"

"He went into Izmir." She didn't elaborate.

"To the museum?" Josh said quickly. A nerve under his left eye started to jump.

Penny found this interesting. "Possibly," she said with caution. "He didn't tell me all his plans."

"I wish I'd known he was going," Josh grumbled. "I wanted to talk with him, and I'd have liked to look in there myself." Penny said nothing, and after a moment's pause he went on, "I suppose he's all excited about those figurines?"

"Oh, so you know about those," Penny said noncommittally. "Who told you?"

Josh was taken aback. "Why—er—it's common knowledge. The young Turk asked me about them when I was down at the station. Wanted to make sure they weren't part of the props. Damned silly question!"

Penny raised her eyebrows. "Oh, really?" Then she added softly to see what reaction she would get, *"In the props or of the props?"*

Josh's eyes swiveled away from her steady gaze. "Told him I'd no idea how Melody got hold of them, and they were probably fakes, anyway. I suppose Toby said the same thing?" His tone was challenging.

"Oh, no, I don't think so," Penny murmured. "But the museum people will know for sure, won't they? I imagine if the figurines are genuine, they'll be of great interest to them."

"Harrumph," growled Josh and was suddenly in a bustle to be off. "Well, tell Toby when he gets back that I'd like to see him." He scuttled out the front door of the hotel, his unopened letters evidently forgotten.

Gloria de Witt appeared next, turbaned and clanking as usual. She swept past Penny with an absentminded "Good day," scooped up her letters with a beringed claw and exited regally up the staircase. Bereft of human companionship, Penny decided she may as well make the best of it and catch up on her own correspondence. Collecting her writing paraphernalia, she made for the lounge, only to find its overpowering smell worse than ever. The deserted dining room was similarly uninviting; so she decided to walk down to one of the open-air cafés and treat herself to a Turkish sherbet while writing her letters, and then she would make another attack on the police station.

An hour later found her happily absorbed in her second lemon sherbet and fourth letter, when a familiar voice broke in on her pleasant preoccupations. "Care for some company, Penny?"

She looked up to find the spare figure of Angus McLean gazing hopefully at her and greeted him with a smile. "Why, Angus—of course! Sit down and have one of these sherbets; they're really very good."

He grinned shyly at her and sat down with a sigh. "Just had another depressing session at the police station, so it's good to see a friendly face. I find that police chief impossible."

"I agree!" said Penny with fervor.

They proceeded to dissect the shortcomings of Hamit Bey for a while, then Angus said, "Where's your friend, Dr. Glendower? It's the first time I've found you alone."

Penny smiled at him. "He went into Izmir to try and get help from the British consul for Gale, poor child. What luck did you have with the American consul?"

Angus shifted uneasily in his chair. "Not much," he confessed. "I'm still waiting to hear from Hy Scrowski, and I don't want to make too many waves in the meantime. It's a devilishly delicate situation for me, as I'm sure you understand."

"Oh, yes," Penny said with some haste. "By the way, there's a letter for you back at the hotel with a Marseilles postmark. Maybe it's from him."

"What a remarkably keen eye and mind you have," he said with admiration.

Penny almost blushed. "Not like Toby's perhaps, but I can pretty well remember the things I want to remember."

"Your very flattering memory of my movies proves that beyond a doubt," Angus said, looking at her steadily.

Penny laughed. "As I said, they are well worth remembering, which is why I recall them all so vividly."

Angus hesitated, then said with almost boyish enthusiasm, "You know, I'm so heartily sick of all this gloom. Why don't we go for a spin in the jeep, up to the old city or somewhere? Just to get away for a bit and talk about things totally unconnected with all this misery and worry. Maybe have lunch out someplace?"

Penny was flattered but also a little taken aback. "That sounds very nice but"—she hesitated—"I *was* going up to the station again to see Bilger Kosay. He's so much more reasonable than the rest, and at least I'd be able to get news of Gale."

"I doubt if it would do much good," Angus said. "After all, I've already tried."

"Still," she insisted, "we could easily swing by there and then go—how about that?"

With some reluctance Angus agreed, and as they drew up in front of the drab-colored building with its red-and-white-crescented flag hanging limply from the pole above the door, Bilger Kosay appeared through the front portal. He stopped with a frown as he spotted them and, before Penny could say anything, said, "I was just coming to look for you, Dr. Spring. There are some matters which we have to go into with you. Would you please come into my office?"

"Can't it wait?" Penny said feebly. "I was just dropping by for news of Gale, and then Mr. McLean and I are going for a drive."

"I'm afraid the drive will have to wait," Bilger said stiffly. "This is of some importance."

"Oh, dear!" Penny looked with dismay at Angus who was also frowning. "I'm afraid I'll have to take a rain check on our expedition."

"I'll wait for you here," he muttered.

"This will take some time," Bilger called out. "I'll see Dr. Spring safely back to the hotel, Mr. McLean. There is no purpose in your waiting."

"What's all this about?" Penny said worriedly as Bilger escorted her into his office and shut the door.

"Where's Dr. Glendower?" he demanded.

"He went into Izmir—didn't Hamit tell you?" she asked with irritation, "He knew all about it. What's happened? Is it something to do with Gale? Has Vincent been found?"

He looked at her sternly. "No, nothing like that." Then, suddenly, he broke into a grin. "I thought you might like to see Gale, perhaps have lunch with her."

"What—here?" Penny gasped.

He shook his head, still grinning, "No. We talked it over yesterday, and she spent the night with the family of one of our constables. She's quite all right and quite safe—both the man and his son are policemen—but none of them speak any English; so she probably could use a little female conversation and companionship."

"Well, I never!" Penny was too dumfounded to question his high-handed breaking up of her tête-à-tête with Angus. "Was that all?"

"No, not entirely." Bilger sobered. "There's still no definite news of Vincent, though we've had reports from both Eskisehir and Baliksehir of 'foreigners,' so they are being checked out. And it may seem a bit academic now, with Vincent in flight, but I thought I'd better tell you that Yamura is also in the clear on the murders, in case you were still hell-bent on detecting."

"Oh? How so?" Penny demanded.

"He came to us yesterday and confessed he hadn't told the truth in his original statement. Seems he's a gambling addict. He got into a game in Izmir, and they directed him to one here in Bergama. As soon as he got here that morning, he went to it and, at the time both the Martin girl and Thompson were murdered, was happily losing money to a pair of our local gambling sharks. He was afraid it would get back to Scrowski, who is very much against gambling of any kind—but now, with Scrowski still absent . . ." He shrugged. "Anyway, his story checks out."

"He wasn't too high on my suspect list in the first place," Penny murmured.

Bilger escorted her out a side door of the police station. "We can walk," he explained. "It's really not very far." They dived into a maze of small streets, so that in no time at all Penny had lost all sense of direction. They stopped before a weathered double door in a blank wall, which opened into a whitewashed courtyard, almost blinding in the bright sunlight. Dazzled, Penny trailed after Bilger's neat back into a long, narrow room opening off the courtyard. She was thoroughly entranced by her first glimpse of a real Turkish household.

The bare interior walls were also whitewashed, as was the long, built-in plaster bench that ran around three sides of the room and which was strewn with brightly embroidered saddlebag pillows and intricately woven *kilims*, providing its only seating. A great brass tray mounted on fragile carved wooden legs stood in the middle of the room, surrounded by more piles of embroidered cushions. Against the fourth wall, and obviously the crowning glory of the whole establishment, sat a small and currently mute television set crowned with a vase of plastic flowers.

In one corner of the bench, huddled forlornly among the cushions, was the small figure of Gale. Two Turkish women of ample proportions sat on another part of the bench gazing at her stolidly. They switched their gaze to Bilger as he entered and greeted him with a flash of gold-crowned teeth, and Gale leaped to her feet with a little cry of gladness at the sight of Penny.

While Bilger was being bombarded with a barrage of Turkish from her two hostesses, she whispered, saucer-eyed, to Penny, "What in heaven's name is going on? What's all this about? I haven't a clue where I am."

"I haven't the faintest idea, either," Penny confessed. "Are you all right?"

"Oh, yes—they keep stuffing me with food and have been very kind—but they do stare so! I can't figure out why I'm here. Last night, as soon as I got through with that villainous-looking police chief, Bilger whisked me out of the station like magic. Is there any news of Wolf?"

"None I'm afraid."

"And what about Dr. Glendower?"

"Gone into Izmir to get help for you." Penny paused. "That *might* be the explanation for this. They may be trying to cut the ground from under his feet if he turns up with the British consul by claiming you're not incarcerated at all."

Further conversation was cut off by Bilger shooing out the Turkish women and advancing on them with a "Well, lunch should shortly be with us, ladies; so make yourselves comfortable." Suiting the action to the word, he made himself a little nest among the cushions on the floor and grinned up at them.

"You're staying?" inquired Penny pointedly.

"Why, yes—even policemen have to eat, you know!"

She exchanged a quick glance with Gale, all hopes of a private conversation now banished, and sat down in a clumsy imitation of Bilger's neatly arranged pose; Gale followed suit with agile grace. Penny decided on the "if you can't lick 'em join 'em" approach and said warmly "I must say, I find this fascinating. I never expected to see a real Turkish home and hearth." Bilger easily took up the conversational ball, and they chatted about Turkish life for a few minutes. Then Penny said with deceptive casualness, "Seeing you here like this brings home to me forcibly something I'm always in danger of forgetting when you're around—that you're a Turk. Your command of English is so remarkable I keep thinking of you as an American."

"Just half," Bilger said with a wry grin.

"Oh?" Penny tried to sound surprised.

"Yes—my mother is American, an American actress, actually. She met my father when on a cultural exchange tour in Ankara."

"And has she completely accepted Turkish life?"

His eyes swept over the bare little room and then back to her. "Well, there are many sorts of Turkish life," he said with a smile. "My father is a lawyer, and life in Ankara and Istanbul is not quite like the life here." His smile grew wider. "And my mother has always kept up her interest in the theater and imparted it to me. So, to answer your next question, yes, I did know several of this present company when they were here before. Would you like a list?"

Happily, the noisy appearance of the women, bearing large trays full of lamb pilaf, home-baked bread and an assortment of preserved fruits and mouth-watering cheeses, covered Penny's confusion. They served Bilger first, as a matter of his primordial right as a Turkish male, which kept him busy for a few minutes while Penny regained her composure, but she wasn't helped by Gale's barely supressed mirth and her whispered "Got you there didn't he, Doctor?"

Conversation passed into safer channels as Penny did ample justice to the excellent lunch. She was happy to see Gale also tucking in with apparent appetite. However, as soon as they had finished their tiny cups of Turkish coffee, Bilger uncoiled himself, held out his hand to help Penny up and said, "Visiting time is over, I'm afraid. I've got to get back to the office after delivering you to the hotel." After a brief good-bye to Gale and her hostesses, he bustled Penny out.

As he dropped her off at the front door, he said warningly, "Now, for pity's sake, stay put here until Dr. Glendower gets back, will you?" Penny watched him go with mixed emotions. She felt she had just been moved and manipulated like a piece in some weird game, the purpose and outcome of which completely baffled her. It was a most unsettling feeling, and she wished Toby would hurry up and get back so she could talk it over with him.

A glance at her watch showed her it was now midafternoon. So far that day she had accomplished precisely nothing, she thought with dismay, and Toby might be back at any moment. Fighting an overwhelming urge to take a nap after such a substantial lunch, she made her way with determination to the Vincents' room, and this time her persistent tapping on the door was answered—after a considerable pause—by a muffled "Who is it?"

"Penny Spring, Mrs. Vincent, may I see you?"

The door opened a crack, and the woebegone face of Carla Vincent peered out. The black eye had now faded to an unbecoming yellow-and-purple bruise but was currently unshaded, and it was evident that Carla had been crying again.

The crack did not widen, and Penny concluded she was not about to be invited in; so she said, "I was wondering if you would come along to my room for a drink and a chat," she dangled her bait. "I have some news of your husband."

The head that had been in the act of shaking a firm no stiffened, and Carla said in a strangled voice, "Oh? What is it?"

"I'd rather not discuss it here. Won't you come? I have some rather good brandy, and it really isn't good for you to be cooped up alone in a worrying situation like this. One has a tendency to brood too much."

"All right," Carla said grudgingly and, easing herself through the crack, shut the door firmly behind her.

When the amenities had been observed—Carla seated in the one sittable chair, Penny perched on the bed, and the brandy duly poured—Penny found herself at a loss as to how to begin. Carla sat mute, gazing at her with beautiful, stricken eyes and sipping almost hungrily at the amber liquid in the thick, bathroom glass—the only one available. "I'm glad to see your eye is better," Penny said at last. "Painful things, aren't they? I've suffered quite a few in my time."

The girl's hand flew in a protective gesture to the discolored eye; then it dropped helplessly away. "A legacy from my departed husband." Her tone was bitter. "Probably the only one I'll get from him."

"Well, that is one of the reasons I wanted to talk to you," Penny said with haste. "I think you may be laboring under some misapprehensions about this whole thing. I've talked with Gale at some length, and of two things you can be certain: he certainly was not going away with her—there was nothing like that between them, this she swears to—and, also, his last words to her were that he was coming back here for you. So please don't judge him too harshly before all the facts are known."

Carla looked down into her glass. "Oh, I knew there was nothing really between him and Gale, though I'm not sure *she* wanted it that way, no matter what she says. But there wasn't that much between him and me, either. If he's gone off without me, I guess I can't blame him too much. I asked for it. Maybe I even asked for this." She touched her eye tenderly. "Wolf is too much of an Indian buck to have his pride hurt in any way. He couldn't get over the fact that I didn't love him."

It took some doing, but with expertise built up through many long years in the jungle and the desert of coaxing intimate information out of unwilling informants, Penny managed to get Carla's story out of her. She told it jerkily, with many pauses at first, but then, as the brandy mellowed and warmed her, she spoke with increasing fluency and speed, as if some long-guarded dam had broken inside of her.

It was a very ordinary, almost banal story. As Carla rambled on, Penny did not find herself warming to the girl, whom she put down as one of those ambivalent creatures swept away by the emotions of the moment and largely unaware of either her own motivations or the world around her.

Carla and Andrew had been students majoring in theater arts at UCLA. After a while they had become lovers and moved into an apartment together; the relationship between them had always been a highly charged, highly emotional, often stormy one. Like so many students of her day, Carla had become involved in militant political activities on campus. This had not suited Andrew, who was apolitical and whose interests were entirely centered in his profession. They had quarreled and separated, and in that separation she had met the magnetic Wolf at a meeting on Indian rights.

"For all that some people around here tell it differently," Carla said with bitterness, "Wolf chased me, not the other way around. He just swept me off my feet. When he was aflame with his cause he was so dynamic he probably could have swept anyone off her feet. Not only that, he helped me get started in my career. He was magnificent, and it was he who insisted we marry, not I." She ruminated briefly. "It was a bad mistake, looking back. Maybe if we'd just stayed lovers, it would have worked out, but once married, well, he became the complete Indian husband, and I just wasn't cut out to be the complete Indian squaw. And then the damned cause became a drag when every single cent we had went to it. I mean, we have nothing, *nothing*."

"And Andrew?"

"I knew Andrew was doing well. Even though he's so young—he's a couple years younger than I am, you know—he's really got it all together, and had from the start. But the movie business is still a big, wide world, and we never ran into one another. Then came this damned picture," she sighed, "and there was Andrew. I know now he got himself into it because of me, but when he first came around, I played it real cool, didn't let on I was glad to see him or anything. Then that bloody bitch Melody showed up, and things went downhill fast. When she started making a play for Andrew, I thought I'd lose my marbles. He'd always said he was a one-woman man, and I guess that's true, but it sure in hell didn't look that way to me for a while." She raised haggard eyes to Penny. "I love him, you know. It's just something I can't help, and he can't, either. And Wolf knew." She gulped, shook her head hopelessly and burst into tears. "Oh, I just don't know what to *do!*"

There was a sharp rap on the door that made them both jump, and a voice called, "Dr. Spring, are you in there?" It was Andrew.

"Yes, I am," Penny called back. "Come in."

The door opened, and he came in, then recoiled at the sight of Carla. His face was drawn and chalk white, the vivid eyes panic-stricken, the long, fine hands twitching with nerves. "Oh," he gasped, "you're here! I went into your room and couldn't find you. I looked everywhere. I—I—" His eyes flashed from the sobbing Carla to Penny, who was looking at him in alarm. "Keep her with you, Dr. Spring, until I get back, will you? It's important." There was desperation in the young voice. Clutching convulsively at his pocket, his gaze still wild, he backed out of the door and banged it shut.

For a second Penny was tempted to follow him, but the now wildly sobbing Carla claimed her attention. It took another hefty slug of brandy and quite a while to calm down the distraught girl. When she was once more in control, Penny said, "Why don't we go for a little walk down to the nearest *tabacci* and get some cigarettes? I don't know about you, but I feel an urgent need for nicotine. Besides, the fresh air will do us both good before dinner." The girl nodded mute assent; she seemed drained now and totally quiescent.

Penny prattled on about her numerous and largely unsuccessful efforts to give up smoking as they descended into the empty foyer, but part of her mind was occupied by Toby's lengthening absence—which had started to worry her—and the extraordinary spectacle young Andrew had presented. *Something upset him badly,* she was thinking as they reached the front door, *and I don't think it was just Carla's temporary absence.*

But they were fated not to get beyond the door, which swung open almost in their faces. A grim-faced Bilger came striding through. His impetus carried him a step beyond them, but he wheeled around and barked, "Dr. Spring, Mrs. Vincent—please! A word with both of you." He marched over to the lounge and, throwing open the door, shooed them into the foul-smelling interior. He closed the door and leaned against it, scanning both their faces with unsmiling eyes. Then he said with deliberation, "We have just arrested a man in connection with the two murders that have occurred. He was caught trying to dispose of this." He produced from his pocket something that caused Carla to recoil with a little moan of horror.

"This is a thirty-eight Smith & Wesson," he continued inexorably, "from which five shots have been fired. We are sure that the three bullets found in the body of Washington Thompson will prove to be from this gun. As to the other two"—he paused, looking at Carla, whose gaze was fixed in terrified fascination on the gun in his hand—"well, we have two members of this company unaccounted for: Hyman Scrowski and your husband, Mrs. Vincent. But I must warn you that things do not look good." He paused again. "You see, the man we have just arrested is Andrew Dale."

Something between a moan and a cry of anguish came from Carla. She staggered forward. "No!" she cried. "No —not Andrew. Oh, please, not Andrew!" Then her eyes rolled up and she fainted.

Penny crouched in shock over the crumpled figure of the girl. She looked up at Bilger. "Has he admitted it?"

"Not so far—he just refuses to say anything." Bilger's face was inscrutable. "But one thing is certain—he looks as guilty as hell!"

CHAPTER 13

"I just don't believe it," Penny said staunchly between furious puffs at her cigarette. "I'm sure he's not the murderer."

"It doesn't look very good for him," Toby mumbled, "Motive, means, opportunity—he had them all. That, plus his own attitude! This refusal of his to make any kind of statement isn't helping him one little bit."

"And it is one of the reasons I still firmly believe him innocent," Penny said. "I mean if he were the murderer, he'd certainly have had some story ready in case he got caught."

"Even after being caught red-handed with the murder weapon?"

"He was covering for someone—possibly Carla. I'm sure of it."

"They may have been in it together. I know that's what the police think, but there is nothing they can do about it for the moment. In the state of shock she's in, she is beyond questioning. I'm afraid you're letting your maternal feelings run away with you, Penny. You know how you are with any young man around Alex's age—absolutely hopeless!"

"That's not true," Penny said heatedly, knowing full well that it was. "Anyway, as you've said *ad nauseam* yourself, *everything* has got to fit, and they still have to explain 'mammoth.' "

"I know, I know." Toby muttered. "I'm no happier about the arrest than you are. If only the young fool would open up. Instead, he just says 'Prove it' in that smart-alecky way of his to every accusation they hurl at him. I'm afraid they'll very soon get tired of the verbal approach and get down to more physical means to get something out of him."

"You mean torture?" Penny gasped in horror.

"No, not bamboo shoots under the fingernails—I don't mean that—but Hamit Bey has a short fuse. Too much of 'Prove it' and he's likely to start roughing up young Andrew a bit." Toby uncoiled himself with a sigh. "Since I think this calls for the Marines, there's no sense in waiting around for my ten-thirty appointment with the American consul. I'll get right off to Izmir and track him down, even if I have to haul him out of his bathtub."

"For two pins I'd go along," Penny said. "But I suppose I'd better stay around as long as I'm needed as Florence Nightingale. With Carla in the state she is in, I can hardly leave it to Gloria, whom she loathes, or Gale—the two are simply not *simpatico*, and Gale is pretty shaken about Wolf's death."

Toby grimaced. "It's nothing I'll forget in a hurry myself." His brow furrowed. "I'd give a great deal to know where the body was hidden and why it had to be moved by my unknown terrified friend of yesterday. But it'll just have to wait until I get back from Izmir. I only hope the police haven't trampled up that gulley too much. I carefully omitted to tell them about my X-marks-the-spot since I have a hunch what to look for and they don't." Penny looked inquiring, but he shook his head. "No time for that now; I'll tell you all about it later." And he loped off.

Toby had risen so early, after a perfectly miserable night, that when he got to Izmir, the consulate was not yet open. He managed, after some coaxing, to get the address of the consular residence from a sleepy-eyed guard and rushed onward.

The consul, looking up from his breakfast, was more than a little confused at the sight of him. "I—er—think we have an appointment later this morning, Mr. Glendower," he said cautiously to the popeyed apparition that had appeared in his dining-room door, undeterred by the efforts of a servant to bar the way.

"It couldn't wait," Toby said, striding in. "Things have taken a much more serious turn, Mr. Tate, and so I've taken the liberty of coming directly to you to ask you to return with me to Bergama. I think, if you will allow me to explain, you will agree."

As he rapidly recounted the bare outlines of the complex situation, Toby studied the man before him: on the wrong side of fifty, big, heavy-set, running a little to fat but still a formidable figure of a man. His face belied his body, being redly, blandly innocent, with guileless blue eyes under a thatch of graying hair. On the whole, Toby found him a distinct improvement on the British consul and hoped he wasn't as naïve as he seemed.

The consul heard him out in silence, then drew a deep breath and let it out with a long, drawn-out 'Phew.' He ran a big hand through his hair. "This is a hot one, and no mistake! First I've heard of it, but, then, I've been away." He looked apologetically at Toby. "Truth is, I'm not up on much of this legal and political business. The regular consul left some time ago, and they got me to fill in until they could find money to send another—budget cuts," he explained. "My real line is farming. Sent out to give the Turks expert advice. I get on fine with the farmers, but those politicians!" He shuddered slightly. "However, something has to be done and fast; so of course I'll go back with you, but it'll take me an hour or so to get organized. I'll have to take care of some things at the consulate and we are short-staffed—budget cuts again."

"An hour," echoed Toby dolefully.

"Yes, I'm afraid so, but we'll take the official car." He grinned lopsidedly. "They won't stop that; so we can drive like hell. I've got to make some phone calls. Have you had breakfast? Help yourself. Make yourself at home." He waved an expansive hand.

"Oh, one thing." Toby shambled to his feet. "Do you have any reference books handy?"

"Reference books?" Tate looked puzzled. "Guess there must be some in our USIS collection. They've been stored in the basement of the consulate since we had to close USIS down."

"Budget cuts?" inquired Toby sympathetically.

"Yeah—always the same story. You're welcome to browse through them. Any particular thing you had in mind?"

"Yes. Particularly anything to do with the movie industry—*Who's Who of the Theater World*—that kind of thing."

The consul grinned delightedly. "Well, you've come to

the right place! My wife is plumb crazy about movies—
collects all sorts of junk about them. It's one of her main
hobbies. Pity she isn't here—she could tell you like a shot
—but she's away shopping in Istanbul." He made a wry
face. "Always at it—never seen such a woman for buying
things." He waved an explanatory hand around the room,
which was indeed crowded with a bewildering assortment
of Turkish bric-a-brac. "Where we're going to put all this
stuff when we get back to our farm in Nebraska I've no
idea. Still, you're welcome to look through her book collection. Come along, she keeps it in her 'glory hole' upstairs, I'll show you."

"Most kind of you," Toby murmured with a sinking
heart. He could envision piles of movie gossip magazines.
"Yes, I'll certainly take a look, but perhaps then I'll go off
to the consulate and see what your USIS might have."

"Sure thing, but you may find what you're after right
here." The consul guided him upstairs and into a light,
pleasant and unmistakably feminine room. Toby sent a
mental apology to the absent Mrs. Tate as he realized that
the piles of tattered magazines he expected were actually
two bookcases full of neatly arranged hardbacks, all sub-
stantive. His eyes lit up. "Very good," he breathed. "This
will certainly keep me well occupied until you are ready,
Mr. Tate."

"Just help yourself," the big man boomed. "I'll be
downstairs in the study opposite the dining room if you
need anything else."

With a satisfied sigh Toby began looking over the titles
and selected a tome, ponderously entitled *Biographical
Directory of World Movie Producers and Directors*. He
settled himself to read, his notebook with the movie-com-
pany list open at his side. He started with Hyman Scrowski, who rated half a page, but, beyond learning that for a
movie mogul Hyman had had an expensive and extensive
Eastern-establishment education—Choate, Harvard and
Harvard Business School—and that he was apparently an
optimist when it came to marriage, having taken the plunge
six times, Toby found no clue to what he was seeking.

He turned to Angus McLean, who rated three whole
pages. About midway down the second page Toby suddenly froze and clamped down hard on the stem of his pipe.

"After the findings of the Un-American Activities Committee were made public, McLean, not having American citizenship, was declared *persona non grata* and was asked to leave the country. He returned to Europe and went on to form his own production unit, Mammoth Enterprises, Inc., which produced one picture, *The Drug Pusher*. This film, while winning considerable critical acclaim, was a financial disaster, and Mammoth Enterprises went into bankruptcy."

So Washington Thompson, that "superjock with a lot between the ears," had tried to tell him everything in *one dying word*. "Oh, my *God!*" Toby said out loud as memory flooded over him.

He remembered them all seated in the hotel dining room and Penny's eager face, seen out of the corner of his eye, saying with enthusiasm, "I think I've seen everything you ever made, and I remember all of them vividly," and then this morning, this very morning, Penny trying to lighten the gloom of the breakfast table by saying rougishly, "I really think I've made quite a hit with Angus, Toby. Yesterday, when he found you weren't around, he was all set for a rendezvous in the ruins, with luncheon to follow, but Bilger broke it up. I gave him a rain check, though."

"Oh, God in heaven, he must think she *knows!*" Toby yelped and, leaping to his feet, raced for the door.

He stuck his head into the consul's study and shouted "I've got to get back right away, Mr. Tate. I can't wait I've just discovered who the murderer is, and my American colleague is in the greatest danger. Come as quickly as you can, and go directly to the police station. I hope to God I'm not too late."

"Wait!" the consul yelled. "I'll call ahead. Who is it?"

"Tell them to get hold of McLean," Toby said desperately, "and to hang on to him till I get there and not to let him anywhere near Dr. Spring. Got that?"

"Got it," said Tate, and he turned back to the phone One of his great strengths was the ability not to ask unnecessary questions in times of crisis.

"Good man," breathed Toby—and ran.

Carla was once more settling into a troubled sleep as the sedation took hold. Penny glanced from the white-face girl to her watch and found it was still only nine-thirty. She felt weary and headachy, as if she had already gone through an entire day, and decided to slip outside for a quick cigarette.

In the corridor a young policeman stood, his feet firmly planted apart, his gaze fixed on the door. Not feeling up to enduring the stolid stare for her brief break, Penny held up a cigarette and then ten fingers. The officer nodded solemn understanding, and she scuttled off down the corridor and stairs, out into the welcome sunshine. There she drew a deep breath, leaned against the wall and tried to keep her thoughts away from what might be happening at the police station.

"Dreadful business, isn't it?" She looked up to see Angus gazing worriedly at her. "The police just make one ghastly mistake after another. I think that chief must be a complete fool."

"So you don't think Andrew is guilty, either," Penny said with relief, "Oh, I'm so glad, Angus. Things look so black for him, but I am *positive* he isn't the murderer."

"Positive?" He looked inquiring.

"Yes. It's maddening, but I'm sure I've got the answer tucked away in my mind. I just don't seem to be able to bring it to the surface. Have you ever had that feeling?"

He nodded silently, then jerked his head in the direction of the upper story. "How's Carla? It strikes me that she knows a great deal more than she's told so far."

"Yes, I feel the same way, but she has been in total collapse since last night, and God knows when she'll snap out of it. The local doctor has her heavily sedated; she's asleep at the moment. Have you managed to see Andrew?"

Angus tossed his head angrily. "No chance! I tried to persuade them to let me talk to him, to make him see he has to say something for his own protection, but the idiots won't let anyone near him."

"Toby has gone for the American consul. Maybe he'll manage to talk some sense into him. They should be back before long."

Angus moved around restlessly. "How about coming for that spin we talked about yesterday? If I hang around here much longer doing nothing, I'll go out of my mind. I must confess that the first two did not concern me all that

much, but then Wolf and now Andrew—it's too much."
His voice broke slightly.

"I don't think I can leave Carla," Penny pointed out.

"You said yourself the doctor had put her out again;
she'll sleep for hours. Besides, we'll come back whenever
you give the word. Please come, Penny!"

"All right—maybe a drive would clear my head. I feel
in a fog," she confessed.

"Good. The jeep's just around back. Want to come with
me, or shall I pick you up here?"

"Oh, I'll come with you."

They got into the jeep, but after Angus had switched
on the ignition, he let out a disgusted exclamation. "Damn!
It's almost empty."

"There's a gas station on the way out of town to the
acropolis; we can fill up there."

"No need. I've got a spare jerrycan in the back; that'll
be enough for where we're going," he said carelessly and
climbed out again.

Penny looked at him in surprise, and a little prickle of
unease ran through her. She looked around the deserted
parking lot and was relieved to see the small figure of Josh
White come stumbling around the corner. He spotted them
and angled over to the jeep, coming to rest against the
front bumper. "Where are you off to?" he croaked.

He looked in terrible shape, red-eyed, unshaven, and his
wrinkled hand resting on the right fender was shaking
visibly, but the bloodshot eyes were still fierce and keen
under the heavy brows. Penny saw that he was dressed in
very old "digging" clothes and was carrying a small knap-
sack. Her interest quickened. "We were off to the acropolis
for a spin."

Josh licked his parched-looking lips, and his eyes turned
toward Angus, who was intent on pouring the gas into the
tank. "That's good. I was going for a bit of a hike," he
said. "I'll hitch a ride as far as you go—save the old legs a
bit."

"Who asked you?" Angus's voice was cold.

"There's plenty of room," Penny said quickly, "but we
don't plan to be gone long; so you'll have to find your own
way back, Josh."

"That's all right," the old man muttered and climbed clumsily into the back seat.

Angus got into the driver's seat, his lips compressed with anger, but he said nothing further as they took off in a cloud of dust. The journey to the old city was accomplished in a heavy silence, which gave Penny plenty of time for reflection. As they bumped up the dirt track past the theater, lying tranquilly silent in the sunshine, she found it hard to realize that no more than a week ago she had basked there so free of care. Now three people were dead, there were two young girls with shattered lives, a young man with his neck in jeopardy, and all of them—young and old alike—had been touched by this deadly blight. She hugged herself against the sudden chill that swept over her. The jeep ground to a stop. "This is as far as we go. Does this suit you, Josh?" Angus's tone was ironic.

The old man opened his eyes and blinked blearily at them. "Oh, fine, fine!" he mumbled. They all got out, but he still hovered uncertainly near the jeep. "Have a good hike, Josh," Angus said firmly. "We're just going to have a stroll around the ruins ourselves."

"Oh, yes. Might take another look around myself." Josh muttered. "Will you be here long?"

"No, not long. Penny has to get back."

He wants to get rid of us, Penny thought. *Toby's hunch must be right. I've got to try and find out where he's headed.*

"Well, we don't want to keep you." Angus's tone was firmly dismissive.

The old man shambled away, muttering quietly to himself. Angus turned to Penny with a wry grin. "I thought we'd never get rid of him. Fond as I am of Josh, he can be a real pain in the neck sometimes. Any particular place you'd like to look at?"

"Just up the hill and around and about." Penny said with an answering smile. He took her arm, and they strolled upward, chatting up a desultory fashion but sometimes lapsing into a companionable silence. *What a pleasant man he is,* Penny was thinking, *so restful to be with,* when a distant noise caught her attention.

"What is it?" Angus demanded as she paused to listen.

"I thought I heard an engine," she said, "It sounded like the jeep for a moment, but I'm probably mistaken."

He looked at her in growing dismay. "Oh, don't tell me Josh has taken it and left us stranded!" he exclaimed. "I thought he wasn't very 'with it' this morning. He does get these spells."

"I don't think he'd do that. I mean, why would he? And, anyway, he doesn't drive, does he? Perhaps it's someone else paying the acropolis a visit. After all, we don't have exclusive visiting rights!"

"Well, if you don't mind, I think I'll just pop back and make sure," he said apologetically. "It would be pretty devastating if someone is trying to pinch the jeep. I'll get the rotor this time, and then we'll be sure they can't. I'll meet you up here. Where will you be?"

"Up there." Penny waved a hand in what she hoped was the direction of the royal gardens. She was anxious to zero in on Toby's fatal gulley. "Don't hurry—I'll be all right."

He gave her hand a little squeeze before he hurried off, and she was left to a silence broken only by the light keening of the wind through the broken columns of the ruins. All trace of the noise that had aroused her attention had now disappeared.

She walked slowly up to the edge of the escarpment and then along it, looking down into the valley below. Had Josh had enough time to make the descent? She didn't think so. He might just be lurking around somewhere waiting for them to depart before going on his mysterious errand. She shaded her eyes and tried to pick out the right gulley. Toby, as usual, had described it in painstaking detail; so she ought to be able to pick out his landmarks, particularly since she was a great deal more farsighted than he.

She sat down on the edge of a sarcophagus, which yawned stonily empty, and lit a cigarette. Up here the wind was picking up, plucking at her red nylon pantsuit with a thousand tiny fingers, and she noted some storm clouds rolling in over the mountains at the far plateau's edge. *I hope we're not in for another storm like the other night's,* she thought anxiously and looked around. Her cigarette was finished, and there was still no sign of Angus.

Wherever could he have gone? she mused uneasily. *He's in such a gallant mood, it's odd to leave me hanging on the vine for this length of time. I certainly wasn't boring him.* She recommenced her strolling, her eyes riveted on the valley below.

She located several Judas trees coming into flower, but no twisted olive to match Toby's description. Finally she spotted what was almost certainly the proper combination and was peering over the edge to see if she could spot Toby's goat path, when she sensed someone behind her. She stepped back sharply from the edge and started to turn. She got a brief glimpse of an upraised arm, a hunk of marble clutched in the hand; then it descended, and in one crashing wave of pain she was spiraling, spiraling downward into blackness.

The murderer crouched over her crumpled body. "I'm sorry it had to be you—I really am." And there was grief in his voice.

CHAPTER 14

When Penny came around, it was to total blackness, and for a heart-stopping moment she thought she had been blinded. Instinctively she put up a hand to her darkened eyes and, in so doing, brushed against stone. She felt it and explored upward to more stone about two feet above her head. She struggled to rise, in spite of the exploding waves of pain shooting through her head, but was somehow constrained. Another sickening fear swept over her, and she hurriedly felt around to establish the confines of her prison. The exploration ominously confirmed her fears. She was lying in a stone box about two and a half feet wide and six feet long. Her would-be murderer had entombed her alive in a stone sarcophagus!

Wave after wave of terrified panic swept over her, and for several minutes she fought desperately to control it, trying to keep from screaming and using up her precious supply of air. *Oh, my God,* she thought, tears pricking her eyes, *why didn't he just finish me off and have done with it; not this, anything but this!* She struggled to reestablish control over her shrieking nerves, trying to fix on something, anything, that would take her mind off her claustrophobic fears. She concentrated on her own pain. She was acutely uncomfortable, lying on something large and knobby; with her one unrestricted hand she felt under her and discovered her large handbag still on its broad leather strap around her shoulder. Gritting her teeth against the pain, she arched her back and wriggled it out from beneath her. Then she turned to what was impeding her movement and found that her nylon jacket was bunched up and apparently caught between the top of the sarcophagus and its lid. The thought gave her a faint flicker of hope that maybe some air could still filter in.

Once more she wriggled and twisted, until she had

slipped her right arm out of the imprisoning jacket, and this small victory heartened her. She groped around again and found wetness in one corner! Her own blood or water? She had to find out.

She fumbled in her handbag until her fingers found her cigarette lighter, and by its tiny flame—surprisingly brilliant in the darkness of the tomb—she examined her strange prison. Sure enough, in one corner by her head was a small puddle of water. At least she would not die of thirst—yet.

She shone the tiny light around and saw, at the foot of the sarcophagus, vine tendrils clinging to the masonry and rooted in the fine layer of dirt at the coffin's base. It told her a great deal. The murderer had obviously enclosed her in one of the great Greek sarcophagi and then had shifted its heavy lid into place. It might even be the very one she had so recently sat upon for her casual cigarette at the edge of the royal gardens.

She hunched up and tried to lever the lid with her feet, but she could not feel the slightest trace of movement. Groaning with the effort, she reversed position and, getting on hands and knees, pressed her back against the lid with all her might. It remained immovable. Panting with the effort and streaming with sweat, she subsided. It was hopeless; she simply did not have the strength to gain her own release. Once more panic welled up, but she fought it down. Now she must hold two goals firmly in mind: to get sufficient air to keep breathing and to keep herself occupied so that she would not go stark raving mad. The rest would have to be up to Toby.

She examined her pinned jacket and pressed her cheek against the small crack to see if she could feel any current of air; none was detectable.

Light—she had to have more light. With the lighter in one hand, she dumped out the contents of her handbag, scrabbling among its voluminous contents until, with a little surge of triumph, she came up with her keycase, a hard Buxton case that embodied in it a tiny flashlight. Offering up a silent prayer that the batteries wouldn't be dead, she pressed the button, and a stronger beam shone out. Thanking heaven for Alexander and his schoolboy's passion for gadgets (it had been a birthday present from him long ago), she put the button on SET and turned to examine the vines at the coffin's foot. Some of them were quite substantial, almost as thick as her little finger, so if they had not been completely crushed by the replacing of the coffin lid, they might provide an air source. She crawled down and pressed her cheek against their dusty leaves, and her heart lifted as she felt a light puff of air: at least for the moment she was all right, she would not suffocate.

Moving her belongings to the airy end of the tomb, she scrunched up and surveyed her store for treasures. She found there were many.

The first order of business was to remedy her throbbing head and to get her thinking faculties back into working order. Her hand went out to the small bottle of Bufferin, and then, using the top of her pen as a container, she scooped up a little of the muddy water to force them down her parched and aching throat. She extinguished the precious light and sat quietly in the darkness with her eyes closed, waiting for the pain-killer to take effect. When the pain had subsided to a dull throb, she turned the flashlight on again and continued the examination of her treasure-trove: a small penknife, which might be useful; a few slightly squashed cookies and some squares of chocolate, remains from her snack in the Egyptian basilica, which she had never got around to dumping out. Now she was thankful for her own sloppiness: with those and the slender supply of water, she could keep going for several days if she had to—though her soul gave a terrified quiver at the very thought.

She looked wryly at her passport and money scattered on the floor of the tomb. How quickly the necessities of civilization became superfluous! They were good for nothing save to supply perhaps a little light when the tiny flashlight gave out.

There was an almost full packet of cigarettes. A sudden longing for the comfort of nicotine swept over her, but she did not know if she dared with the slender supply of air. Perhaps she could increase that supply.

She looked speculatively at the vines and then at her penknife. If she could get some of them loose, perhaps she could pull them out and make a hole to the outside world.

It would mean using a lot of the precious light, but it might be worth it. On the other hand, it could result in settling the lid more firmly than ever, cutting off the precious supply of air altogether. It was a gamble, but one worth taking, she decided. At least it would give her something to do.

She looked the vines over and decided to attack three stout ones in the middle, leaving the ones at either end intact. Until she got to the crack, she could work without light and so again plunged herself into darkness. She scrabbled away, using the cigarette lighter from time to time to see how she was progressing. It was simple until she got to the lid, because its great weight pressing down had so compressed the vines that she could get them out only a thin sliver at a time.

Time dragged by as she patiently gouged on, but no additional puff of air or glimmer of light rewarded her efforts. When the penknife was all the way into the crack and there was still no sign of a breakthrough, she was near despair. "I need something else, something longer," she muttered frenziedly and went back to her stores. Her slender gold Cross pen was no longer than the penknife, so she discarded that, but there were several plastic Bic ballpoints that would give her an extra inch or two. They would have to do, since they were all she had.

She began to jab away with one of them, forcing it deeper and deeper into the hole. When there was too little of it left to get a grip on, she removed a shoe and, using the heel as a hammer, drove it all the way in. *If it breaks, I've had it,* she was telling herself grimly, when she felt a sudden lack of resistance. Excitedly she dropped the shoe and, seizing another of the pens, poked at its mate, now completely invisible in the hole. For an agonizing moment nothing happened; then her heightened sensibilities sensed rather than heard the first pen fall free. Withdrawing the second, she was rewarded by a tiny shaft of light that shone into the tomb like a welcoming beacon. She regarded the small shaft of sunshine with more triumphant satisfaction than she had felt since they had first placed Alexander in her arms. To celebrate, she treated herself to a cigarette.

She leaned against the stone side of her prison and

watched the blue smoke swirl in the tiny beam of light and for the first time allowed herself to think about her attacker. Who had it been? Angus, who had brought her here and who had known exactly where she was? Josh, who had been so oddly insistent on coming with them? Or the unknown driver of the car whose engine she had heard? She realized she did not have the faintest idea. She could not connect that upraised arm and its weapon of death with any one of them.

Another thought struck her. What if Washington Thompson had also been caught, as she had been, totally unawares? That last word of his—the one she and Toby had put so much stock in—might have been, as Bilger had once said, just the meaningless babble of a dying man. He may have had no more knowledge of who had put three bullets in him than she had now of her assailant. All this time they may have just been chasing rainbows.

"There will be rainbows but no pot of gold," Gloria had said. The strange words danced in Penny's mind, making no sense. With a sigh she shook herself out of her reverie and stubbed out the cigarette, which was now burning her fingers. *Well, this won't do any good at all—so back to work!*

Now I need to make some kind of signal, she thought. *What can I use?* She eyed her scarlet jacket, hanging incongruously against the side of the tomb. It was a good eye-catching color, but how could she work the limp fabric through the minute hole? She needed something long and stiff that she could fasten scraps of the material to and push through; "a banner with a strange device," she muttered wtih grim amusement. Her passport had stiff paper —perhaps if she tore the pages into thin strips and twisted them together . . . She picked it up and, in so doing, disclosed something that brought forth a yelp of gladness. Several slightly grubby pipe cleaners were revealed.

Now, how in the world did those get in there? She regarded these unprepossessing objects with a fond eye. She must have collected them in some now-forgotten cleaning up after Toby, who had a small genius for leaving things behind in hotel rooms. *They'll be the very thing!*

She cut some small scraps out of her jacket lining and

with clumsy fingers attached them as firmly as she could to the pipe cleaners; then she went to work on a new hole.

It took even longer than the first, and by the time it was finished, she was thoroughly exhausted, her head once more swimming with pain. With trembling fingers she inched her pathetic little banner through the new hole, and when she was sure it had reached the outer air and was anchored in the hole, she leaned back with a great sigh. *I've done all I can. Now it's up to Toby.*

She allowed herself the remnants of the chocolate, some more Bufferin and another tiny sip of water. Now would come the hardest part of all—the waiting.

Time I found out if I learned anything from that transcendental meditation course—God knows it cost enough! I might try some ESP on Toby. If ever he's going to find me, he'll need all the help he can get, she thought grimly and, closing her eyes, began to concentrate fiercely on sublime nothingness.

Such was Toby's state of anxiety that he recalled nothing between the time he flung himself out of the American consul's home and his precipitate arrival at the hotel. He had accomplished the trip in record time, leaving in his unheeding wake a long string of apoplectic and shaken Turkish drivers.

All the way, he had tried to tell himself that his fears were groundless, that he would return to find Penny quietly at her watch beside the sick girl. However, one look at the stricken white face of the young policeman outside of Carla's room told him that what he had most dreaded was now fact.

The young man stammered at him, "She just said she was going out for a cigarette. Ten minutes, she said. Kosay Bey was very angry with me for letting her go, but how could I stop her, *effendi?*"

"He has been here?"

"Yes, *effendi,* been and gone. She is not in the hotel— he looked."

"And who else is here?"

"Of the foreigners? Only the women and the Japanese. The rest"—he shrugged miserably—"I do not know. I was told to stay here, and here I stayed, but Kosay Bey could not find any more. He said the jeep was gone—"

Toby turned on his heel and raced back down the stairs, passing an equally white-faced and startled-looking constable in the lobby. He flung himself into the car and roared off to the police station.

He found Hamit pacing back and forth in his office like a restless bear, his face a thundercloud. "Where the hell is Kosay?" Toby roared at him.

Hamit stopped his pacing, his body hunched forward with angry tension. "That's what I'd like to know," he roared back. "After I got that crazy phone call from the American consul, I sent him with a constable to bring Dr. Spring back here. Next thing I know is the constable phones me from the hotel to say he is stranded because Kosay has taken off in the jeep without him and that there is no sign of Dr. Spring. I don't know what the devil Kosay thinks he is up to, disobeying orders like that."

"Why the flaming hell didn't you bring in McLean," Toby yelled, going into a fine Celtic fury. "Didn't you understand what Tate was telling you? He's your murderer!"

Hamit became dangerously calm. "I cannot go around arresting people just on the strength of some wild idea of yours. We have our murder suspect in custody. I was bringing in Dr. Spring just as a personal favor to you. Why on earth should McLean want to harm her?"

"Because he thinks she knows what Thompson's dying word meant," Toby snarled. "He's the one involved in the drug racket. I can prove it now. But this is not the time to explain; every second counts. We've got to get after them. Get every man you have and come with me." His temper had flared out to be replaced by an icy calm.

"What's the rush? If it is as you say, she is already probably . . ." Hamit began but was silenced by the terrible look in Toby's eyes. Instead he said hurriedly. "Yes, well, we'll do it your way," and rushed out, shouting orders, Toby in close pursuit.

Minutes later a convoy of cars was roaring back toward the hotel. "Why there?" Toby shouted over the noise. "One party should be sent at once to the amphitheater, the other to the acropolis. If he lured her out, those are the two most likely places they'd have headed. We're wasting time going to the hotel."

"I've got to find out where Kosay went," Hamit said stubbornly. "It'll only take a minute."

They screeched to a halt at the front door of the hotel, and Hamit rushed up to the young constable waiting on the steps. "Kosay Bey—what did he say? Which way did he go?"

"He said nothing, *effendi*. He just ran past me and took off in the jeep that way." The policeman waved a hand in the direction of the old city.

Hamit muttered an oath and got back in the jeep. Just as they were pulling out, a small figure catapulted through the hotel doorway. "Wait!" called Gale. "I'm coming, too." And with incredible agility she leaped into the moving jeep.

Hamit turned angrily. "What the devil does she think she's doing? This is no place for a woman," he barked.

She leaned forward to Toby. "If Dr. Spring is missing, I want to help," she said fiercely, her wide nostrils flaring. "And you can tell that old devil I can outrun, outsee, outsmell and outtrack all his damn constables put together. Too right I can." She leaned back panting.

"Let her come," Toby said quietly to the fuming chief. "We need all the help we can get. How long ago did Kosay take off?"

Hamit glanced at his watch. "Almost two hours ago."

"So they were gone before that—how long before we don't know," Toby said and groaned in despair.

Hamit threw him a sympathetic glance. "Where do you want us to start?" he said as the hill of the acropolis loomed into view.

"We'll start at the theater. It seems the focal point of the whole affair," Toby said tightly. "Have one group of your men fan out from it down the hill and another search upward. Tell them not just to look for—" he boggled at the word—"a body, but for anything out of the ordinary— a stone overturned, a cigarette butt, paper—*anything*." He repeated what he had said in English for Gale's benefit.

"McLean doesn't smoke," she volunteered.

"No, but Penny does."

"Oh?" She sounded surprised. "I've never seen her with a cigarette."

"She's been off them for months but went back to smoking last night—she does when she's upset—and once she starts, she smokes like a chimney," Toby said quietly.

They were at the theater, and in seconds the silent tiers were swarming with an army of brown-uniformed ants; every tier, every passage, every hole was investigated with no result.

"Nothing," Hamit reported, panting. "Which section will you go with, up or down?"

Toby looked despairingly around. The ruins offered a million hiding places, and Penny was so small, so very small. "I'll go up," he said in a strangled voice. "All right, then, I'll take the other way," Hamit said, and for a brief moment his hand rested on the stooped shoulder of the taller man.

The brown-coated horde was swallowed up by the gray ruins, and a strange silence fell, broken only by the wailing wind and an occasional rumble of thunder from the dark clouds now sweeping down over the hill, blotting out the sun. Toby looked up at the grayness, willing the clouds to hold back their burden until his quest was complete—for better or worse.

A sudden shout broke the silence, and he and Gale ran in its direction. She easily outdistanced him, and he arrived to find her facing two policeman across a crumpled khaki-clad figure on the ground. "It's Josh," she announced.

Toby knelt and turned over the small figure. There was no mark on him, but as Toby moved him, Josh gave a soft groan. Toby seized him by the shoulders and shook him roughly. "Josh! Josh! Where are they? Where did he take her?"

The old man opened a dazed eye and murmured feebly, "Tried to keep an eye on them. They went up—I was following. Must have circled round me behind me somehow . . . knocked me out. . . ." He closed his eyes again.

Toby said rapidly to the policemen, "Get the rest and start searching from the top of the escarpment back in this direction. If you find anything, report back to me."

He waited until they were out of sight and then seized

Josh again, shaking him until the older man's teeth rattled and Gale let out a horrified, "Don't—you'll kill him!"

"If he doesn't tell me what I want to know, you are so right," Toby said between clenched teeth. The old man's eyes opened in alarm to meet his deadly gaze. "Now," Toby hissed, "I don't give a damn what game you've been up to, Josh; you're going to tell me exactly where you found Vincent's body. Was it a cave, a tomb, what? It's the most likely place he'd have taken her, so talk or, by God, I'll wring your scrawny neck right here and now."

Josh shook his head feebly, and Toby bunched up the neck of the old man's shirt and twisted it until Josh choked. Gale tried to pull him off, but he brushed her aside. Finally Josh gasped, "All right, all right," and Toby relaxed his viselike grip a fraction. "Talk," he hissed again.

"A tomb." The old man rolled his eyes wildly. "You'd never find it without me—tomb of Puduhepa. Greatest find . . . tablet . . ." His hand fumbled at his pocket. "Make us famous, Toby—you and me. Secret?"

"Never mind that now," Toby snarled. "I know it's somewhere up that gulley, but is it sealed? How did you seal it?"

"Tried to frame me," the old man rambled on. "Didn't know he knew. Must have followed . . . Vincent's body in the shaft . . . put the stone back . . . gray-white like all the rest but"—he gulped—"a green vein running through it—marble. Our secret, eh, Toby?"

Toby dropped him with an exclamation of disgust and wheeled on Gale, who was looking at him in horrified fascination. "I'm going down there," he said. "You go on up to the top with the rest and see what you can find."

"But what about Josh? He needs help." She pointed a trembling finger at the supine figure on the grass.

"Later," Toby snapped. "He'll survive, and even if he doesn't, it won't be much of a loss." He loped off.

The gulley showed traces of the police invasion, but Toby hurried on beyond the small valley in which Vincent had been found to the little cairn of rocks he had left. Anxiously scanning the rocks on both sides, he continued up the narrowing ravine. It took a sudden twist as he rounded the corner, and dead ahead a gray-white boulder slashed across with a vein of green marble met his anxious

eyes. For an instant he paused before it, half dreading to
find what lay beyond; then he put his shoulder to it and
heaved.

A gust of clammy air, laden with the smell of ages,
greeted him as he stooped and scurried into the narrow
shaft. Despite the dim light, he could make out where
Vincent's body had lain and the imprints in the dust of
several sets of boots. But of Penny there was no sign, even
though he pursued the narrow passage up to the point
where it had been blocked completely by a barricade of
small rocks. With a sinking heart he retraced his steps. He
had been so sure that this would be the place, but now . . .

He emerged from the gulley and lifted miserable eyes
to the outline of the acropolis. A small figure that had been
standing immobile on the edge of the escarpment suddenly
erupted into frenzied movement. Gale was waving at him
frantically. He scrambled rapidly up the goat path and was
soon at her side, panting. "What is it?" he gasped.

"I found this," she exclaimed delightedly and opened
her dusky palm to disclose a cigarette stub. "I found it
over by that old empty tomb, and it doesn't belong to any
of the policemen; they aren't allowed to smoke on duty."

"Is that all?" he said in disappointment.

"No, it's not." She took an eager sniff at the battered
stub. "I've smelled this somewhere else on the acropolis. I
was waiting for you because I had to make sure it wasn't
yours."

"Not mine." He produced his pipe from his pocket and
proferred it to her with growing eagerness.

She sniffed at it like a hungry dog and shook her head.
"No, it wasn't that. Come on!" He swiftly followed her as
she made her way through a jumbled maze of fallen walls
and columns. Then she froze and exclaimed, "There! I've
got it again." She turned slowly in a complete circle, her
broad nostrils flared wide. "This way!" She hurried on.

Toby uttered a choked exclamation as something red
caught the corner of his eye. He wheeled, and there, sticking incongruously out of a carved stone tomb, was something like a miniature red-and-white barber's pole. "Over
here," he yelled. "Quick! Help me with the lid."

In a bound he was at the side of the stone coffin. It's
lid was slightly askew. He bent with all his might against

it. The lid moved with grating protest, and he was gazing down at a small huddled heap, the tousled mouse-colored hair matted with blood. Overcome with faintness and grief, he leaned against the tomb. Then, suddenly, the head moved and the hazel eyes, screwed up against the light, opened and looked up at him.

"It's about time you showed up," said Penny. "I was down to my last cigarette."

CHAPTER 15

So much had happened all at once that the principals involved were still trying to sort out themselves and their sudden wealth of information.

Penny had stoutly resisted all efforts to ship her off to Izmir and a big hospital. "I'm damned if I'll go, not just when all the action is getting started." Compromise was reached when, after X rays had shown that her skull was not fractured but that she undoubtedly had a concussion and should be in bed, she was installed in a local clinic in a tiny two-bed ward all to herself. There she startled the nurses by demanding that the windows be opened as wide as possible. "Air," she informed them groggily, her eyes slightly crossed, "is one of our most undervalued and precious possessions," and slid into a solid twelve-hour sleep.

Toby, to celebrate her escape, had retired to his room in the hotel, got quietly and thoroughly drunk and passed out for an equal amount of time. So both were blissfully unaware of the exciting developments that were taking place all around them.

Josh had been examined by a doctor who found nothing but a small lump behind his left ear. Now he, too, lay in sedated sleep back in his hotel room under police guard.

Although there was a hue and cry now for McLean, both Josh and Penny had added an element of doubt when they stated that they could not positively identify him as their assailant and that they both had heard another car on the acropolis shortly before they were attacked.

Of McLean and Bilger Kosay there was still no sign, and the hunt for them was not helped by the fact that shortly after Penny had been lifted from her tomb, the heavens opened and the deluge was still continuing, turning dirt roads into bogs, tarmac into streaming rivers.

Mr. Tate had finally returned to Izmir, but not before he and, surprisingly, Gloria de Witt, had demanded and been granted an interview with Andrew Dale. What transpired at that interview was unknown, but, as a result of it, the recalcitrant Andrew announced that if he could talk with Carla Vincent, he would be prepared to make a full statement.

Hamit, going quietly crazy in the absence of his English-speaking assistant, had had to send off to Izmir for an interpreter, and it was not until the early hours of the morning that Andrew's statement was made and Hamit was free at last to snatch a few hours of sorely needed sleep.

So, between Morpheus and the continuing rain, all were unaware of another significant development that occurred when a small, slight figure slipped quietly into the sleeping hotel in the dawn's early light.

Toby, not feeling his sprightliest, decided to skip breakfast and go directly to the clinic. He found Penny propped up in bed, her bandaged head with tufts of hair sticking out wildly between the bandages making her look like a demented Martian. She was regarding a laden breakfast tray with the utmost satisfaction.

"Hello," she greeted him cheerfully. "You're looking a little peaked this morning. Hang one on last night?"

He grunted.

"Here"—she rummaged on the bedside table—"take a couple of these—do wonders for an aching head. After all, since you put me out of my misery, the least I can do is alleviate yours a little." She proffered two white tablets.

He swallowed them obediently but grumbled, "You owe more to Gale than to me."

"Without your pipe cleaners I would have been forever lost."

"How in the world did you happen to have them?"

"I don't know—cleaning up after you somewhere, I suppose." They grinned at one another suddenly.

"Feeling better?" he said.

She nodded and started to crunch on a piece of toast. "What's new?"

"Well, I'm not exactly up to date, but I had a session with Josh last night that cleared up quite a few things and put another nail or two in McLean's coffin."

"Oh, dear!" Penny shook her head sadly and winced. "I just hate to think it's he. He's such a nice man; why on earth would he want to kill me?"

"Because of your much-vaunted knowledge of his works," Toby said, icicles on his voice. "He thought you knew his own production company was called Mammoth and its only product his film called *The Drug Pusher*. Obviously you hadn't put it all together, but he couldn't take the chance that you would."

"So *that's* what I had at the back of my mind," Penny said thoughtfully. "You know, now that you've said it out loud, I remember it perfectly. How stupid of me! How did you find out?"

"Reference books," Toby barked. "As I said at the start, if I'd followed established scholastic procedure and checked my basic sources first, a man's life might have been saved."

"Well, it wasn't exactly an obvious clue," Penny mused. "Why on earth didn't poor Thompson say McLean and have done with it?"

"It just shows you that you should take everything into account," Toby said ponderously. "Thinking back, Thompson *was* obviously trying to get his name out. He was mouthing another *M* when he did, and I falsely assumed he was going to repeat 'mammoth.' He was trying to give us not only the murderer but the motive as well."

"If they were mixed up in the drug racket, I can see why he murdered Thompson, but why Melody?"

"I don't think he did murder her," Toby said surprisingly and held up a restraining hand as Penny let out an exclamation. "Wait! I'll give you the reconstruction of things as I see it, but first let me tell you what I got out of Josh last night."

Penny buttered another piece of toast and leaned back to listen.

Toby began, "I had to drag most of this out of him, but he had pretty well gone to pieces; so I think this is the straight story. It goes back to the last time they were here. Josh was snooping around for antiquities, and the word soon got out. A pair of brothers, local men, brought him the gold figurines, and, of course, Josh knew at once he was onto something special. After a lot of bargaining, they brought him some more stuff, including a cuneiform tablet, which leaves little doubt that the tomb they've been filching the stuff from is the tomb of the Hittite princess, Puduhepa—a daughter of one of the earliest Hittite rulers, who was married off to a prince of this area. She's already known as being one of their earliest royal troublemakers; so you can imagine what a priceless find this is.

"Anyway, Josh went to McLean, whom he thought he could trust, told him he was onto something big, borrowed some money from him to bribe the men to show him the tomb and gave him the gold figurines as collateral. Josh persuaded them to lay off the site with promises that they'd strike it rich when he came back with a full-fledged expedition. According to him, when the murders occurred, he was checking up to see that they hadn't been monkeying around with the site in his absence. He claims that McLean dropped him off on the road and then said he'd continue looking for shooting locales and would pick him up later, which he did. And McLean agreed when the news of the murder broke that he'd alibi Josh. It didn't occur to the old fool that *he* was providing an alibi for McLean."

"So you don't think Josh was mixed up with the drugs?" Penny queried.

"He swears not, and he was petrified when the figurines turned up in Melody's handbag. Then, when he returned to the tomb and found Vincent's body there, he was equally terrified that someone had discovered his secret and was trying to frame him for the murders, and that's why he moved the body."

"But he doesn't directly accuse Angus of this?"

"No. He thought perhaps Andrew had somehow tumbled to the secret, had done away with Vincent because of Carla and had hidden the body there because he thought Josh could keep quiet about it. Josh was convinced of this after the gun business."

"I have an idea on that," Penny said slowly. "I think, supposing Angus *is* the one, that that was a plan of his that miscarried. He was most upset about Andrew's arrest;

so I think I know what happened. He planted the gun in *Carla's* room, hoping that she'd be blamed for all three deaths: she was jealous of Melody, and Wolf had been beating her up. But I think Andrew went into her room the day she talked to me, found the gun, leaped to the conclusion that his ladylove was guilty—that would account for the awful state he was in when he came to my room—and decided to take the blame on himself when he was caught trying to ditch it. Angus is genuinely fond of the boy, you can tell that; so I think this misfire threw him off-balance."

"As I see it, he's been acting in near panic all the way along," Toby agreed. "I don't think any of the murders were actually planned: he got boxed into a corner and so has been forced from one act of desperation to another. Although there's still a lot we don't know, and may never know, I think the sequence of events went like this.

"Thompson was assigned either to make a pickup or a contact with a drug peddler in Izmir. Melody, who had been on the snoop, caught him in a weak moment and got him to show her the secrets of the camper. McLean, having dropped off Josh near his site, returned to the hotel for a rendezvous with Thompson, only to find him high as a kite on drugs and Melody smugly displaying the figurines, which McLean must have had hidden in the camper.

"Somehow he must have dissembled, got them to change into their costumes for some 'mock-ups' and driven them up to the theater. There he must have put the fear of God into Thompson and told him to get rid of the girl and meet him later at the amphitheater. Thompson got rid of the girl as ordered, but then *didn't* get rid of you. When Angus learned this, he just couldn't take the chance of a 'hophead' like Thompson being apprehended, and so he had to get rid of him, too. Unfortunately for him, Thompson didn't tell him where he'd hidden the body; so he couldn't retrieve the figurines."

"But, then, why kill Vincent?"

"Because, just like Thompson, Vincent must have been in on what the camper was for and what it contained. He may have guessed what had happened but was too deeply involved himself to do anything about it. Then I think McLean started to get nervous about Gale and what she might know. As you found out, Wolf Vincent felt very protective about her. So he made a last desperate try to keep them all uninvolved by sending her away with the camper, hoping no doubt that she'd get away and the authorities here would eventually assume she was the guilty party and would not pursue the matter when they couldn't find her. Then he went hunting for Angus, caught up with him on the acropolis, told him what he'd done and that he was cutting out as soon as he could—and got shot for his pains.

"I surmise at that point Angus might have tried to put the blame on Josh for the murders and lured Wolf up that gulley to show him the site. Then he planted the gun on Carla."

"It certainly all fits in," Penny said with a gloomy sigh. "I wonder if Andrew was involved at all."

"I'd like to know about Scrowski," Toby said.

Penny polished off the last morsel of food and leaned back. "When I was stuck in that tomb in all that fug, it occurred to me that the nasty smell in the hotel lounge might well stand investigation—it just might be Scrowski!"

"Well, wherever he is, if he's alive, he has a lot of explaining to do," Toby observed.

"I'd much rather have him the villian of the piece than Angus," Penny sighed.

The door opened, and the frowning countenance of Hamit appeared around it. "Oh, there you are," he barked at Toby. "Could I trouble you for your services as interpreter again? The man they've sent from Izmir is a nitwit, and I want to go over some points in Andrew Dale's statement once more."

Penny caught Andrew's name and said eagerly, "Ask him if Andrew's off the hook, Toby. I do hope so."

Hamit came all the way in as Toby repeated Penny's question. "It has to be checked out, of course, but it looks as if the young fool was only trying to protect Mrs. Vincent. He claims now that he found the revolver in her room, and since we know that room was clean the day before, it does look like a plant." He hesitated. "We've had a lucky break. Remember the hotel in Istanbul that Vincent sent the Australian to? We rounded up some very interesting characters there, including one from Izmir who escaped our net in the last sweep and who we thought had skipped the country. He's been singing loudly to the Istanbul police and was the contact Thompson had met that day in Izmir. He has named Thompson and Vincent and says there's a big man behind them whom he never met—a syndicate man." Again he paused.

"American syndicate?" Toby queried.

Hamit nodded. "It was as we thought." Toby grinned to himself as Hamit continued, "They were planning to get the raw opium moving again into Europe. They packed it in cylinders, and that camper would have held enough of them to keep the refineries busy for a year." He was interrupted by a harassed-looking constable sticking his head around the door and urgently beckoning to him. "Come *in*," Hamit said with asperity. "What is it now?"

The policeman rolled a nervous eye at Toby and stammered. "Report from the village of Dimde, *effendi*, on the Baliksehir road—two jeeps in a ravine and two injured men, one in a bad way. They're bringing them in now."

Hamit muttered a string of Turkish oaths under his breath and made for the door. "You'd better come with me," he called over his shoulder to Toby. "One of them might be McLean!"

Penny was left alone with her thoughts, but not for long. There came a tapping on the door, and the turbaned head of Gloria de Witt appeared around it. "May we come in?" she asked roguishly. "I have a surprise for you, Dr. Spring! Someone is *very* anxious to meet you. I want you to meet Hyman Scrowski and his new bride!"

Penny watched in stupor as a small, elegant man edged into the room. He was accompanied by a willowy blonde who was a good six inches taller than he and a carbon copy of Melody Martin. His soulful black eyes swept expertly over Penny, assessing and dismissing her as a sex object, as he glided forward with an outstretched hand. "So very happy to make your acquaintance, Dr. Spring," he said in a surprisingly deep, Harvard-accented voice.

"Wasn't it naughty of Hy," Gloria continued, a trace of acid in her voice, "running off and getting married and not letting us know any of his plans. I've told him all about the terrible time we've been having and what a help you have been. He's just too *sick* about it all—aren't you Hy?"

"Yes," he agreed absently, and then said, "I'd like you to meet my wife, Genevieve. Say hello to Dr. Spring, Genevieve."

"Hello," the blonde said in a sultry whisper.

So much for my smell in the lounge, Penny thought but said aloud, "Now that you're here, I hope you'll help to clear up this ugly mess, Mr. Scrowski."

"Oh, please call me Hy!" He unveiled a charming smile. "Yes, indeed—as quickly as possible." He switched his attention back to Gloria. "There's no hope of salvaging the film now. Vincent can't be replaced in a hurry, we don't know if McLean will be available, and Brett wants out to marry his gay divorcée—just as well, since his face has gone completely to pieces and I don't think we can use him again—and though Genevieve could take Melody's part"—he gave his bride an appraising glance—"I think the whole thing is just too difficult, don't you agree? We'll just take the whole thing as a tax write-off: with this murder business, the taxmen won't make any waves, and we'll also be able to collect on the insurance." Gloria nodded and clanked agreement, the blonde yawned, and Penny felt sick.

"How about Carla and Gale?" she asked faintly.

Hy looked at her in surprise. "Oh, I can always find a spot for Carla—good enough little actress and a pretty face. As for Gale"—he shrugged—"I suppose we may find her another bit part, but I'm not sure it's worth it."

"Their husbands have been *murdered,*" Penny said sharply.

"Oh, yes, a great pity," Hy said with haste. "But I'm so glad Andrew didn't do it. I'd hate to have lost him. Never seen a boy who can turn his hand to so many things. Hope they haven't given him too hard a time: he's such a nervous type."

Penny looked at him in disbelief: not a monster as she had imagined him, but a monster even so. "If you don't mind, I am still far from recovered myself; the doctor does not like too many visitors."

"Oh, quite so! Well, so happy to have met you—er—Dr. Spring." He started to shepherd the women out.

"Just one question before you go, Mr. Scrowski," Penny called. "Why Marseilles?"

"Marseilles?" He turned in surprise. "Oh, as European headquarters, you mean? My first wife had an estate there —excellent for all kinds of location shots, and so on—and a lot cheaper than Paris." He smiled briefly at her and was gone.

"Oh, *boy!*" Penny exploded as the door closed. "I hope Hamit gets hold of him and really puts him through it."

She felt completely drained and soon fell into an uneasy sleep. When she awakened, the shadows of afternoon were already lengthening, and Toby was bending over her. "Penny," he whispered, "I don't know if you feel up to it, but they've brought them in, and Bilger has been asking for you."

"Is he badly hurt, then?" she asked anxiously.

"Bad enough—a dislocated shoulder and a fractured leg —but it's McLean who's in a bad way with a broken back and pelvis, and lying out in that pouring rain all night hasn't helped either of them."

Penny groaned.

Toby helped her along to another room as white and as clean and bare as her own. Bilger's face against the white pillow looked darker and sunken, but as Penny entered, the dark eyes opened and he grinned faintly. "Hi, our indestructible lady. Just wanted to see you to apologize." His voice was drowsy.

"Apologize? To me? Whatever for?"

"For being a lousy policeman, for not following my hunches, and for not being quicker off the mark." He rolled his head from side to side. "I was keeping a pretty close eye on you, because I had a hunch about McLean, but I never thought he would move so soon. I suppose he was getting pretty desperate. When I found you had gone, I went straight to the old city, but, like a fool, I wasted time searching in the theater. By the time I finished, he must have buried you in that tomb. I heard his jeep start and chased after him. It was a real James Bond chase—my mother would have been proud of me"—he swallowed and winced—"but with a bit of Charlie Chaplin thrown in, too. I got a flat, and McLean must have had to stop and gas up somewhere. Anyway, I chased him a good seventy miles before I caught him. I tried to cut him off, but by that time the rains had come and I couldn't control the jeep, and we both went over the edge." He closed his eyes. "The irony is that my revered chief now thinks I may have had a hand in all this. And the funniest part of all is that, when we were both lying out there waiting to die, McLean told me the whole story, and Hamit doesn't believe me. If McLean dies . . ." He didn't finish that. "I just wanted you to know that I wasn't mixed up in it, that's all." His eyes closed, and his head sagged sideways on the thin pillow.

"Oh, my God!" Penny gasped. "Is he dead?"

Toby shook his head. "Just passed out again." He looked quizzically at her. "Do you believe him?"

"I—I think so," Penny stammered.

"Hamit doesn't, and for once I'm inclined to agree with him. If McLean dies without talking—if there isn't something to back up his story—Bilger is going to be in one hell of a tight spot."

CHAPTER 16

"For once I bring naught but tidings of great joy," boomed Toby, striding into Penny's hospital room, rubbing his hands with glee.

Two days had passed, and Penny, now sufficiently recovered, was bent over a suitcase, busily packing.

"I always knew Hamit was a man after my own heart," Toby continued. "He took as much of a dislike to Scrowski as you did and, I gather, has been leaning on him pretty hard. He didn't say so, but I think he must have hinted that he would confiscate the camper if Scrowski didn't come across and do things his way. So, faced with the possibility of losing a forty-thousand-dollar piece of equipment, Scrowski has agreed to underwrite Gale's trip back to Sydney and to ship Wolf's body back with Carla to the States. Apparently Wolf was very big with the Blackfeet, and they are going to bury him with full tribal honors.

"Andrew is going with her. He has decided he's had enough of this outfit and has already had a couple of job offers. Scrowski's fit to be tied! I suppose Andrew and Carla will get together now, though I must say I rather agree with you about the girl—not much substance there. Still, if it's what he wants. . . .

"Even Josh, the old rascal, is getting off lighter than he deserves," Toby rattled on. "The director of the Izmir museum is so delighted with the new tomb that he has persuaded Hamit not to press charges. So Josh will just be fined for the figurines and allowed to leave, though he'll be barred for life from Turkey. You'd think the old goat would be grateful, but not he! When last seen, he, Scrowski and Gloria de Witt were sitting around with faces as long as fiddles, going over the accounts and grousing.

"Gale left on this morning's plane and said to tell you good-bye, that she'd never forget you, that she'd write, and that she'll never ever take a walkabout again, once she gets to Sydney.

"Oh, and I've got us booked on a flight out of Izmir tonight, which will get us into London in plenty of time for me to pick up my formal duds from Moss Brothers and make my bow to the queen on schedule."

He stopped, becoming dimly aware for the first time that something was very amiss. Since he had entered the room, Penny had not uttered a single syllable, nor had she as much as glanced at him.

He walked over and peered down at her. "Good Lord!" he said with awe. "You've been crying! What on earth is up?"

Penny raised reddened, puffy eyes to him. "I went to see Angus."

"You *what!*" It came out as a yelp.

"I *had* to. I had to find out for myself. If he died without speaking—" She choked up and went and sat in misery on the edge of the bed. "One of the doctors here speaks English; so I took him along as a witness—that should be good enough even for Hamit." She swallowed hard, and two more tears spilled down her cheeks. "Oh, Toby—it was terrible! He looked so small and *broken*—so incredibly pathetic."

Seeing that she was about to break down again, Toby, who was panic-stricken at the sight of tears, said sternly, "He caused the death of three people and would have killed you, so less sympathy and more substance. What, if anything, did he say?"

"Oh, he told me the whole story," she said wearily, "and it was more or less as you had reconstructed it, but at least I found out a few more of the whys.

"It seems that it all began after the Americans kicked him out. Some of the money to finance his film company came from the 'clean' side of the syndicate. When he went broke, they were very decent about it, didn't pressure him or anything. Wild isn't it? Over the years he has done them one or two small favors, like smuggling in sable coats from Russia among the company props for Mafia wives, but nothing big at all. Then, when the big drug ring was cracked in Izmir, they asked him a bigger favor—to help get things started again. He wasn't too keen to do it, but

they dangled a fat financial carrot before him and Wolf
Vincent—they both needed the money—and allowed them
to fix up the camper. But whatever Angus and Wolf were
supposed to do, evidently they didn't do it very well; so
the syndicate increased the pressure and insisted on sending in one of their own men—Thompson, of all people!—
over whom they had complete control. It does not say
much for their organization if they trusted someone like
him, but I guess even they have their blind spots.

"Angus was glad to be off the main hook, but he became pretty nervous when he realized how unstable
Thompson was. He came back that day to check if all had
gone well at the 'meet' at Izmir, only to find Thompson on
a way-out trip and Melody looking like the cat that swallowed the canary." Penny shook her head and gave a bitter
little laugh. "All that gobbledygook we went through at
the start of this thing about theories and motives—God,
how ridiculous! There were no plans, no real motives—
just human panic, panic feeding on panic.

"When Angus got them up to the old city that day, he
made Thompson see that Melody had to be silenced.
Thompson knew very well that if the syndicate found out
what he'd done, it would put his life on the line; so he
went along. He just planned to intimidate Melody into
keeping her mouth shut, but then she panicked and ran,
and he knifed her in the passage leading to the stage at
the theater.

"The killing must have sobered him up a bit, I think,
though Angus didn't realize that Thompson hadn't any
idea where he was, because of his recent shot of drugs.
Thompson must have come out on the stage with the body,
seen me sitting, dozing, up in the seats and tried to sneak
up behind me to knock me out before I saw the body.
Then he would have had time to dispose of it. When he
reached my seat, I had already gone down to the stage.
At that point he must have realized that it was too late,
that I'd found the body. He just didn't have the heart to
come after me and kill a stranger in cold blood. Instead he
hid the body after I started out for town, and then he went
off to meet Angus as prearranged. Angus, when he heard
there had been an eyewitness (though Thompson didn't say
who it was—I, like a fool, told him that!), realized that

the police would be bound to find Thompson and that he'd probably spill everything, especially if he were locked up for a while, and—well, the rest you know."

"But why did he kill Vincent?"

"Panic again. Vincent believed McLean's alibi at first—just as we all did. Then, when Melody's body was found, he began to get panicky, because he knew that the figurines had been in the props and only he, McLean and Thompson knew that. He dreamed up this scheme to get Gale and the camper out of the way, hoping the police would think her guilty but would let it go at that after she had escaped. He set up a meeting with Angus at the old city, told him what he had done and said the whole affair was getting too rich for his blood, that he would take whatever money there was on hand and split with Carla. Angus realized that Gale probably wouldn't get clear of the country and, also, that Vincent had sent her to one of the hideouts of the drug ring. He needed another suspect quickly; so he made up some cock-and-bull story about Josh being the murderer because of the tomb. He offered to prove it to Wolf, took him there, murdered him, walled him up and sat back.

"He thought the police would fix on Vincent as the number-one suspect—as they did—but when Josh panicked on finding the body and then you found what he'd done, all McLean could think of doing was to try and fix it on Carla—and then *that* misfired. He was at his wits' end, particularly when I kept babbling on about his films, and he was sure that sooner or later I'd remember—" She broke off again and shook her head sadly. "I asked him why he had left me to such an unmerciful death, and he said he just couldn't bring himself to hit me again—that he liked me too much! That's what's so terrible about this whole affair—he has so many *good* qualities."

"So, on the evidence, did Thompson, Melody Martin and Vincent," Toby said dryly, sensing the threat of another torrential outburst, "and so, for that matter, do you. As far as I am concerned, I'll keep my sympathy for the victims, not the murderer."

"But he's *dying!*" Penny wailed.

"I know." He did not add that it was the most merciful thing that could happen to Angus, since, if he lived, the

Turks would undoubtedly hang him. Instead he said, "It is probably the best way out."

"But all that brilliance!" Penny moaned. "What a waste. What a pitiful waste! And you know how I hate waste."

"Hmph," Toby grunted. "And what of Bilger?"

"He had absolutely nothing to do with it. It was just as he said," Penny said drearily. "So you were all wrong about him. Thank goodness, he's going to be all right." She got up and snapped her case shut with a decisive bang.

"I seem to have been wrong about a lot of things," Toby agreed with gloom. "I must say, as a detective I appear to be a bit wanting. Perhaps I should stick to archaeology. And speaking of that, we've got just enough time for me to get back a little of my self-esteem by giving you the scientist's tour you should have had ten days ago." He looked at her hopefully.

Penny gave him a wan smile. "Oh, I don't know, for a first try I don't think we did so badly as detectives. with my brains and your charm, we might yet go far!"

He grinned and shook his head at her.

"And, yes, a very *short* scientist's tour would be just fine with me." She picked up her camera. "I want to make one last trip up there to get some shots of my Greek saracophagus."

"What in heaven's name for?"

"To send to Alexander. He'll be thrilled. After all, it isn't *everyone's* mother who has been entombed and risen from the grave! I feel like something out of Edgar Allan Poe."

"That's gruesome," Toby mumbled, picking up her bag and making for the door, "positively gruesome." He held it open for her. "You know what you are?" he said to her retreating back as she went out. "You're Gothic—pure American Gothic." And he followed her, grumbling happily.